A SOLDIER'S DESTINY: EAGLE SECURITY & PROTECTION AGENCY

BEYOND VALOR BOOK 6

LYNNE ST. JAMES

A Soldier's Destiny

Copyright © 2019 by Lynne St. James
Cover Art Copyright © 2019 by Lynne St. James
Published by Coffee Bean Press
Cover by Lori Jackson Designs
Created in the United States

 Created with Vellum

A SOLDIER'S DESTINY

Delta Force Team member, Jasper "Raptor" Ramsey was in the wrong place at the right time when he pulled an injured woman from the carnage after a terrorist attack in Paris. But before he could find out her name, his unit was activated and he had to leave without knowing her fate.

After terrorists ripped her world apart, Aurora "Rori" Prince abandoned her life in Paris and returned home to Willow Haven, Florida. She tried to put the past behind her, but someone doesn't want her to let it die. When she and a very pregnant Lily Barrett barely escaped injury in the latest attempt against her, she finally admitted needed help. Turning to Chase from ESP, he assigned one of his best to be her protection.

When Jasper gets his new assignment, the last person he expects is the woman he'd given up hope that he'd ever find. Now he has a second chance, but can he keep her safe and earn her love?

DEDICATION

For all those who have suffered at the hands of terrorists at home and abroad.

For T.S., my hero.

PROLOGUE

P*aris, France – November 13, 2015*

After the mayhem of their mission in Syria, it was a relief to hear laughter and happy chatter, even if he didn't understand most of the conversations. It was Friday evening in Paris, and fate had given him an eight-hour layover to decompress on his way back to the states. He sure as hell wasn't going to complain about the downtime.

Fancy food wasn't his usual preference, but since it had been over twelve hours since his last meal, the gurgling in his stomach was getting insistent that he eat something soon. The flight attendant said he'd love the food at *La Belle Équipe*. No matter what the menu contained, the thought of sitting down at a table to eat a real meal instead of the MREs he'd been feasting on for the last four weeks was heaven. Now, if he could just find the damn restaurant he'd be set. He was double checking the location on his phone when he heard a familiar sound. Too familiar. But not one he'd expected on the streets of Paris.

There was no mistaking the sound of machine gun fire. It shredded through the happy chatter like mini-explosions followed by terrified screams. The buzzing of the bullets tearing through the air prompted Jasper "Raptor" Ramsey into action. After he checked his six, he set off to locate the shooter or shooters. The rapid fire of the guns echoed in his ears. Terrified people pushed and knocked each other down as they tried to escape the madness. The chaos.

Following them to safety wasn't an option. Instead, Raptor ran toward the pandemonium. As he moved through the hysterical crowd, he worked on a plan to handle whatever he'd find. It was what he did. It didn't matter that he wasn't on a mission, he'd do what he could to help.

As he rounded the corner onto the *rue de Chaconne*, he found the source of the shooting. Bodies were strewn across the terrace of the restaurant. Moans and screams echoed in his ears as he arrived on the scene.

The police arrived as he did, and as they exchanged fire with the gunmen, Raptor maneuvered his way onto the terrace to check for survivors. It was as bad as any mission he'd been on with his team, and he would have been thankful for their help. But the Deltas rarely traveled together. To say they were secretive would be an understatement. Even most of their families didn't realize they served on the elite team. And for now, he was on his own.

Moving from body to body, he checked each one for a pulse before moving on to the next. The first three he encountered were already dead and he was beginning to think he wouldn't find any survivors. Then he heard a faint sound.

"*Aidez-moi, s'il vous plaît.*"

Turning toward the soft female voice, he stepped over the debris that was strewn across the terrace and searched for the woman. When he finally got to her, she was covered in blood and half-pinned beneath a table in the corner. Without knowing if it was her blood, he was careful not to make any sudden moves that might release pressure and increase the bleeding. Gently, he lifted the table from her lower body to assess her injuries.

Not sure if she was French or not, he struggled to recall his high school lessons. A bad joke for sure. Languages weren't his strength, and he left that to Wolfman.

"Madame, *vous* okay?"

"I can't move my leg but it's burning," she answered in English. *Thank God*.

"You've taken a couple of bullets in your calf. You're in shock right now, but you'll be okay," he answered as he pulled a cloth from one of the tables and ripped off a strip and tied it around her thigh to help slow the bleeding. She'd been lucky if you could call it that. Her wounds weren't life-threatening, but they'd still hurt like hell.

"Can you please help my parents?" Her voice was weak but steady and he was impressed she was calm.

"Where are they?"

"My mom is there." The woman pointed to an older female lying about five feet away. "I don't think she's breathing. My dad's over there, I think? He's not moving either. And I can't find Jim."

Two fingers to the woman's neck told him she was already gone. She'd never had a chance based on the bloom of blood in the center of her chest. The older male on her other side had several bullet wounds, but the headshot had probably been the one that had killed him. There was nothing Raptor could do for her parents, but he was determined to make sure she survived.

Her blue eyes were filled with desperation and pain, as he laid the tablecloth over her parents. It was so raw it forced him to look away. He couldn't imagine what she and all the other injured were feeling at that moment. They weren't used to this, shouldn't have to be, it's why the teams put themselves in harm's way— to keep attacks like this from happening.

"No...please, help them. They can't be dead." Her heart-wrenching plea was a stab in Raptor's chest. But there was nothing he could do.

"I'm so sorry." He was, he didn't know her or any of the dead or injured lying on that terrace, but it didn't stop him from caring, although he'd never admit it to anyone. His hard exterior hid the scars he'd kept from everyone in his life. Most people he met thought he didn't give a shit about anyone, but it was his armor. If he didn't let anyone in he wouldn't be hurt. There had been enough of that in his childhood.

The police dealt with the last of the gunmen and were separating the injured for triage and questioning the uninjured that were still in the vicinity. The bleating sirens from the approaching ambulances replaced the sounds of machine gun fire.

"Sir, please. Can you help Jim? He was... Oh. My. God." Her face crumpled in horror. Raptor turned to see what caused her reaction. It was the other person she'd been searching for, he'd been revealed as the police moved an adjacent table. Half of the man's head was missing, his remaining eye was open and staring, a look of shock forever captured on his face.

Raptor moved to block the sight, distracting her, though she'd never really forget what she'd seen. But he hoped that it wouldn't be her final memory of him, whoever he was to her – boyfriend, brother – it didn't matter. "They're going to take you to the hospital."

A small blood-covered hand reached out and he grasped it in his. His hand looked huge cradling her tiny one.

"Thank you for helping me." Her voice broke as she tried to hold back her tears. The medics lifted her onto a gurney, and it was time to let her go, to see if there was anyone else he could help. Except he didn't want to let her go. Something drew him to her. It made no sense, but it was there, the feeling that he was meant to help her, to be with her, to protect her.

But there were others who needed his help and he released her hand and stepped back. As she was wheeled away, the sense of loss almost took his breath away. He should have asked for her name, and where they were taking her, to make sure she was going to recover. It sounded false even to his own ears but didn't matter, it was too late. She was gone.

"*Es-tu blessé?*" one of the officers asked as he grabbed his arm.

The question took him by surprise until he

looked down at his bloodied shirt. "No, it's not my blood," he answered in English. No sense in trying to use his piss-poor French.

"*Bien*, good."

As he continued to check for survivors and helped triage the wounded, his phone buzzed. Very few people had his number, and without looking he knew it was his team.

Report in asap. We've got new orders.

It didn't surprise him, especially when he'd heard from the police that the restaurant hadn't been the only location hit in Paris that evening.

CHAPTER 1

W*illow Haven, Florida – Present Day*

The buzz from the Fitbit on her wrist reminded her it was time to open the bakery. As she took one last look around the now immaculate kitchen area, Aurora "Rori" Prince, flipped the from closed to open and unlocked the door to let in the small group of people lined up along the sidewalk.

Her second favorite part of the day was about to start, the first was creating the treats that brought her friends and neighbors into Prince's Patisserie. When she'd opened the bakery a bit over a year ago she had hoped it would do well. With a Walmart just outside of town it had made it a gamble. But her little slice of Paris on Main Street had exceeded all of her expectations.

It wasn't how she'd expected to use her culinary certificates from the *Cordon Bleu*, but that one night in Paris had changed everything.

Everything.

Rori had planned to make Paris her home after she graduated. She'd had grand plans of opening a little shop and growing old with Jim. But in mere moments on the horror-filled evening, she lost everyone she loved. Devastated. Alone. She'd been broken mentally and physically. It took much longer to heal than she'd imagined, and when the doctors finally discharged her from the hospital, she'd come back to Willow Haven. Paris was no longer the place of her dreams. That one night had transformed it into a never-ending nightmare that played on repeat whenever she closed her eyes.

Willow Haven hadn't offered her the comfort she'd hoped to find. The house was too empty, too full of memories of her parents. The ache of never seeing them again, never hugging her mom too long and too tight, never again hearing the quiet laughter her parents had shared tore open the wounds that had just started to heal. They were gone.

Then there was Jim's loss which was even more devastating. They had their whole lives ahead of them. First graduation and then dinner with everyone she loved. The night had been filled to overflowing with joy. She'd felt like the fairy princess her parents had named her after. Then Jim proposed adding the ganache to the cake. But seconds later the gunfire started, and he was gone too. All of them stolen by fanatical terrorists who'd wreaked havoc throughout Paris.

The chime over the bakery door pulled her from her reverie.

"Morning, Rori." She looked up to see Lily Barrett come through the door and smiled. It was impossible not to. One look at the very pregnant Lily in her pajamas and fuzzy slippers was all it took to start her day with a wide smile.

"Hey, Lily. How are you feeling? I can't believe you just don't call me to bring you whatever you want. Should you even be driving?"

"I'm fine. The doc says the baby will be here

in two weeks. I'm taking him at his word. Alex and I tried for so long. We never thought it would happen. Now that it has, I'm terrified I'll be a shitty mom."

"You will not. You've been blessed with this baby. I've seen you with Chloe's girls, you're great with them. It's just new mother nerves."

"Probably. Thank you. You're a blessing and so is this bakery. I don't know what I would have done to satisfy my cravings without you. Alex tells everyone I'm not really pregnant just stockpiling eclairs." Lily giggled and rubbed her protruding baby belly.

Rori laughed too. Alex and Lily had been through their own hell and back. They deserved to have some happy now. "I don't think that's possible. Maybe you should ask him if he's going to give birth to a croissant."

"That's a good idea."

"Do you want your usual?"

"Umm, maybe make it four eclairs today…"

Rori turned back to give Lily a look with the open bakery box in her hand. "Four? Maybe I should make it a half dozen just in case?"

Lily's cheeks turned a little pink, but she nodded with a sigh. "Am I that bad?"

"No, you're pregnant. I was only teasing. But it is the first time you said four."

"I know. But they're so fucking good. I could probably eat a dozen."

"I bet once you have the baby you'll never eat an éclair again."

"Oh, I'll take that bet. No way am I giving these suckers up."

"We'll see. Did you want anything for Alex?"

"Yeah, two croissants for him, and a few of the macarons for Chloe. She's coming over to help me finish putting together the baby's room."

"Sounds like a wonderful morning."

"It would be better with coffee. It's the one thing that has been fucking killing me. Chloe said it doesn't taste good when you're pregnant. I think she's telling me that to make me feel better. How the fuck could coffee not taste good?"

"I threw in a couple of extra eclairs for later," Rori said with a wink as she handed over the little pink cardboard box tied with a black bow. Pink and black were the signature colors of Prince's. It reminded her of the happier times in

Paris, and she needed to hold on to those otherwise it was all just blood and death. It would be too easy to let that night turn her into a bitter person, but her parents and Jim wouldn't have wanted that.

"You're too good to me. Seriously, Rori, I'm so glad you came back here after everything and not just for the eclairs. I just hope that we've helped you heal at least a little in the last year."

"You have, more than you know. Knowing my friends are there for me has meant the world. I still have some bad days, and I miss my family, but it is getting better."

"Good. Now I guess I better get the hell back home before Alex wakes up and realizes I'm gone again."

With a wave, Lily turned to leave, but before she got close to the door, the plate glass window at the front of the store shattered. Shards of glass flew through the air, raining down on the interior of the bakery. Without hesitating, Rori ran out from behind the counter and pushed Lily behind her to block her from injury.

～

"**D**ammit, Raptor. You can't punch the client because he's wrong. They hire us to protect them not put them in the hospital."

"He had it coming, Chase. He's lucky I didn't take his fucking head off."

"No, you're the lucky one. If you don't chill out, you're going to find yourself stuck behind a desk. Do you hear me? Anger management classes, bro. I'm not kidding."

If Raptor heard he needed to "chill out" one more time, he really was going to kill someone. Didn't they realize that his life, his family had been stolen from him? Being Delta was what he'd been born for, trained for, lived for. The injury then medical discharge still didn't seem real. He had no idea what to do with his life now and babysitting a bunch of pansy-assed rich people was not a satisfying career choice.

The last mission had been a huge clusterfuck. They'd been ambushed, a real shit show. By the time the smoke had cleared in an unnamed location on a mission that didn't exist, two team members were dead and three were injured, including Raptor. Even with all of that, they'd successfully rescued the HVT, and gotten everyone the fuck out of there.

It shouldn't have gone down like that. Bad intel happened more times than not, but it had gone south as soon as they'd reached the rendezvous point. As the shit hit the fan, shrapnel exploded taking him down. As he lost consciousness, he was transported back to Paris, the woman's haunting blue eyes pleading with him, not to save her parents, but to hold on.

After that, she'd shown up in his dreams most nights. Her voice calling to him. He was beginning to think he was losing his mind. When the damage to his leg was too severe to return to his Delta team he felt lost. His focus deserted him. Keeping his emotions hidden wasn't as easy, and his cold and calculating demeanor had a huge crack in it. His lack of emotion had earned him the nickname Raptor. It was part of him or had been, for as long as he could remember. But Paris had been the start of the change for him. Then the injury. And now he had to wonder if he'd ever get his head out of his ass. After two years of searching with no luck, he needed to admit he'd never find her and move on.

"Raptor, dammit, are you listening to me?"

Chase Brennan demanded. Nope, that was a negative. He'd been too busy reminiscing about a past that didn't matter anymore. He was losing it. Maybe, his boss was right, and he should talk to someone.

"I am now."

Chase shook his head and cursed under his breath. Raptor was saved from whatever scathing retort was coming when the phone rang.

"Brennan."

It was his chance to escape the butt-kicking, and Raptor might be slow, but he wasn't stupid. Hoping for a clean getaway, he stood up to leave, but Chase stopped him with the wave of his hand and pointed to the chair he'd just vacated.

While he waited for Chase to finish his call, his mind wandered to the mystery woman he'd saved in Paris. She probably would have been found by the paramedics in time even if he hadn't been there, but he liked to think he'd been the one to save her.

If he was honest with himself, he'd admit that she'd been a distraction even before he'd been injured. Maybe not as much as afterward but thoughts of her would pop into his head at the worst possible moments and steal his concentration.

Hoping that if he located her and learned she was okay, he'd be able to move on, he'd started searching for her. After every mission, he'd try to find her, but it was like she only existed in his dreams. If it hadn't been for the bloody t-shirt he'd been wearing that evening, he might have doubted his sanity. Why he'd saved it, God only knew because he sure as hell didn't. Every time he went to toss it in the trash something stopped him. And now, two years later it was stuffed into the back of his dresser drawer. It lived there until he felt the need to feel her presence, then he'd pull it out and look at it.

"Is she okay? Any leads? Yeah, I agree, but Alex is going to have a coronary. No shit. I'll send him over to help her board up. No problem. Thanks for letting me know, Steele. Talk to you later." Chase disconnected the call and made some notes on the laptop. Then turned to Raptor. "I have a job for you."

"But I thought..." Raptor swallowed his

protest, he'd much rather be working than stuck behind some desk. "Great, who am I babysitting this time?"

Chase rolled his eyes before he answered. "That was my brother, Steele. You've met him at my house a few times I think. Anyway, this time you get to stay in town. The woman who runs the bakery is having some trouble. Today it escalated and Lily Barrett, Alex's wife, was injured."

"Fuck. Is she okay? She's pregnant right?"

"Yeah. She's at the hospital now, but Steele said she seemed okay, mostly shaken up. Aurora Prince is your assignment. She runs the bakery and after talking to her, Steele thinks she needs protection."

"I'm supposed to babysit some old lady who runs a bakery? Fuck, man. What kind of trouble could be so bad that she needs protection? It's Willow Haven."

"Listen to me. You seriously need to take a minute and think about what you want to do with your life. You were a good soldier, but you can't be that person anymore. We've all been there. That's why I started Eagle Security and Protection Agency. For men like us, who have to start over, have to find a reason to go on. So, you can either get rid of the chip on your shoulder or you can get the fuck out of my office and keep on walking. This is your last chance."

Chase's words were a rude awakening. Raptor had pushed him too far. He'd done him a favor by giving him a job—a second chance. And all he'd done was cause trouble. "I'm sorry, Boss. I'll be on my best behavior. Scout's honor."

After another eye roll, Chase continued, "Okay. Then head over to Main Street. The bakery is Prince's Patisserie and it's two doors down from the Treasured Tales book store."

"I know the book store, but I don't remember the bakery."

"She opened it about a year ago. I guess you haven't been around town much since you've gotten back."

"Not really. I haven't even gotten an apartment yet." Chase shook his head.

"Well, the other guys are probably going to hate you for pulling this assignment. The woman is a wonderful baker. Everything we've tried has been freaking amazing. Faith loves her macarons. I think half the people in town signed up for gym memberships after she opened."

"I don't have much of a sweet tooth. I think I'll be okay."

"I bet you'll change your tune after you try anything she has in that bakery. Even so, she's the assignment and Aurora Prince is a sweetheart. Just remember that. The woman couldn't hurt a fly if she tried and has been through a ton of shit. So be nice to her."

"I said I would."

"This case is important, she's beloved by everyone in Willow Haven. The bakery is busy all the time and the last thing we need is anyone else getting hurt. So, if you have any hope in hell of redeeming yourself, this is the time."

"Yes, sir."

"I mean it. Don't fuck this up."

"Understood. Thank you for giving me another chance."

"You're welcome, Jasper. Keep your cool and you'll be fine. Since the job is in town you have plenty of back up if you need it."

"I will."

It wasn't until Raptor climbed onto the back of his Harley and tightened the strap on his helmet that it hit him. Chase used his name. No doubt he'd done it on purpose to underscore his point. But it'd been a long time since someone worried about his well-being. Now he had to prove that he deserved it.

CHAPTER 2

Ten minutes later, Raptor stopped at the curb in front of Prince's Patisserie. The pink and black striped awning made it look like someone had transported it from the streets of Paris. The memory of tear-filled blue eyes filled his mind as he pulled off his helmet. Would he ever stop thinking about the woman? He wasn't even sure that she'd survived. Shaking his head to get rid of the memory, he focused on the two cops nailing plywood over what should have been a plate glass window.

At the sound of the bike, they turned toward him. "Did my brother send you?"

"If you mean Chase? Then yes. I'm Raptor Ramsey."

"I'm Steele. I've heard about you from my brother," he said as shook Raptor's hand.

"I'm Ethan Price." Raptor looked around. Nothing looked out of the ordinary except for the broken window.

"Do you know any more than Chase told me?"

"No. I told him everything she said in her statement. I'm not sure that's all of it, though. Call it cop intuition. I have the feeling she's holding back. But maybe you can get it out of her at dinner."

"Dinner? I thought I was supposed to be undercover."

"You are. Since no one remembers you around here, it'll be easier for you. She's at Alex and Lily's house. I'll drop you off."

"Can't I take my bike?"

"You're undercover, remember? You're a distant cousin just out of the military and came to help out with the bakery. You wouldn't have a bike with local plates. If you need to drive anywhere, you can use the bakery delivery van. But since it's at Alex's house right now, I'll drop you off and Ethan will stash the bike at his house."

"I don't know jack about anything in the kitchen, except that it has fire. It'll be a tough sell that I can help out."

"She'll take it easy on you, she didn't exactly want a bodyguard."

"Why does she need one?"

"Apparently, someone's been targeting her for the last three or four months. It would have been better if she'd told us before it escalated to this. But she said she thought it was her imagination until the brick came through the plate glass window and almost killed her and Alex's wife, Lily. I think you know him, at least."

Raptor nodded. "Yeah, I know Alex from ESP. But Chance said they're okay, right?" Innocents being injured twisted Raptor's guts into knots. It was one more thing that had gotten worse since Paris and the blue-eyed woman.

"Yes, they're fine. Rori took the brunt of it, but it wasn't too bad. She ended up with some cuts on her arms as she tried to shield Lily. They were lucky."

"Sounds like it. Any clue who's targeting her or why?"

"That's the problem. It doesn't make sense

that anyone would. The town is small, and as far as we can tell she doesn't have any enemies."

"Wouldn't just closing the bakery for a while be a better idea than taking chances?"

"You'd have riots on your hands. Wait till you taste one of her macarons. Holy crap. I swear every time Anna comes home with one of those pink and black boxes I'm in trouble," Ethan answered.

"It's just a bakery. Seriously?"

"Just wait." Steele laughed. "C'mon let's get you over to Alex's house. I need to get back to the station to file the report. Ethan, you've got the bike, right?"

"Yeah. I'll take good care of her. No worries," he said as he took the keys from Raptor.

Steele's words worried Raptor as he gazed out the window at Willow Haven. Who would want to hurt her and why? How the hell was he going to be able to figure out who was trying to hurt Aurora Prince? He pictured some sixty-year-old Betty Crocker type. Chase couldn't have given him a mission further than his last if he'd tried. Going from stuck-up rich asshole to elderly baker would be different that's for sure.

"Chase said you were injured. I guess it won't affect your ability to do the job?"

"Not at all. I could have stayed in, just not doing what I was before."

"And that was?"

"I can't tell you. I'd have to kill you."

"Ah, it's like that, huh?"

"Yeah. Broke my leg in three places and they had to do two surgeries to get the shrapnel fragments out of my thigh. It didn't heal well enough to requalify and I didn't want to be a desk jockey or an instructor, so I took the medical discharge."

"I hear you. It's a pretty common story with most of the guys Chase has hired. He saw a need and is trying to fill it. I watched him struggle when he first took his discharge. I worried he wouldn't come out of it, but then he started ESP and it gave him a purpose."

He understood what Steele meant all too well. It was like the person he was when he was part of Delta Force didn't exist anymore; he wasn't good enough for anything.

"Anyway, what else can you tell me about the bakery lady?"

Steele laughed. "You'll meet her soon

enough. We're about two minutes away. By the time you finish dinner, you'll hopefully know more than we do."

"Great." *Not.* Aurora even sounded like an old lady. She probably pissed off some teenagers in town. But a job was a job. "At least I know Alex, so it won't be quite as awkward."

"Right. My only advice is don't push her too hard. You're there to make sure she stays safe since we can't give her round the clock protection. Your priority is Rori, let Ethan and I solve the case with the rest of the Willow Haven PD."

"Gotcha. Any other rules I need to know?"

Steele shrugged. "Only the one about not hurting Aurora and keeping her protected. But you know that already. Just tell me what gear you need, and I'll pick it up from Chase and drop it off when we come by tomorrow. I'm assuming you're carrying now?"

"Of course. Do you want to see it?"

Steele laughed. Raptor wasn't trying to be funny but damn the way they spoke about the woman it was like she was some kind of saint or something.

"Any questions?"

"What am I supposed to do? Just walk around glued to her side?"

"You'll probably be sweeping up flour and waiting on customers. But I guarantee that after your first bite of a chocolate éclair you won't give a damn. You'll be infatuated and will do whatever she asks."

"Sweeping up flour? I'm going to be her janitor?"

"More like a jack of all trades. Unless they came up with a better idea."

"Got it." This was going to be a cake-walk, pun intended. Better than another asshole with his head up his ass. He grinned. He'd do his best to charm the pants off the little old lady, find the person who was giving her a hard time no matter what Mr. Detective told him. Then when he was done, maybe he'd go back to Paris and try one more time to locate his nymph. Having a plan made him feel better. But then again, what did they say about the best-laid plans?

Nervous would be a gross understatement. Shaking, sweaty palms, and her stomach crampy, Rori was way beyond nervous. All she knew about her new bodyguard, the one she didn't want, was that he was retired military. But that could mean anything. Why had she let Lily and Alex talk her into this? The window had probably been an accident. Why would anyone want to hurt her? She was nice to everyone and there wasn't even a competing bakery she'd driven out of business. It had to be kids pulling pranks.

"They'll be here any minute."

"I should never have agreed to this. It's stupid."

"No, it's not. You could have been killed. Fuck, we both could have been killed. I don't want to be afraid to go into the bakery worrying that someone will try something else." Lily had a point. She could never forgive herself if anything had happened to her, or anyone else. There'd been enough pain and death in her life. The memories of Paris, the smell of blood and death had taken months to go away. Now it all came flooding back and twisted her up in a knot. She'd lost everyone she loved that night. In the beginning, right after the attack, she'd wished she'd died too. But the man who'd come to her aid had saved her for a reason, she had to believe that she lived for a purpose. She'd wished more than once she'd found out who he was.

"Do you know him?"

"No, I don't but Alex does a little," Lily said. "When Steele called his brother Chase at Eagle Security and Protection, he said Raptor was the best at what he did. What that is I'm not sure and Alex won't tell me. But he's convinced he'll keep you safe."

CHAPTER 3

Steele pulled to a stop in front of a two-story coral colored house. It fit right in with the rest of the quiet neighborhood. As Raptor stepped out of the car, the hair on the back of his neck stood on end. It was the front side of dusk, but still light enough to check out the neighborhood. It looked peaceful, typical of the Willow Haven sub-divisions, and a hell of a lot better than the jungle. So why was his body on full alert?

"Are you coming?" Steele yelled as he walked toward the front porch.

"Yup, on my way." He hadn't been around a lot of little blue-haired women, so maybe it was the reason for his trepidation. Hell, his team would be laughing their asses off if they ever found out. Good thing they wouldn't.

He caught up to Steele as he knocked on the front door. Alex must have been waiting for them since he opened the door while leaning on a cane, almost as soon as they'd knocked. An aroma of deliciousness wafted toward him, and his stomach growled. Alex laughed and winked at him. "Just wait, you ain't seen nothing yet."

Lily came up behind Alex and smiled. Even though Chase had told him Lily was pregnant he hadn't thought about how far along she might be, and she looked about ready to have the baby now.

"You must be Jasper, or do you prefer Raptor?"

"Either is fine, ma'am. I've been Raptor for a long while but I promise I will answer if you call me Jasper."

"You got it. I'm Lily, Alex's wife. But you already knew that, right?"

"I should have done the introductions. I was talking about you on the way here so I figured he'd know," Steele said as they followed Lily and Alex.

"C'mon, let me introduce you to Rori." Lily

took him by the hand and impressed him with her strong grip, which usually meant confidence. He doubted he'd get the same from the bakery owner.

"Don't worry, she won't bite." Alex laughed as he and Steele followed behind them.

"It smells delicious." His comment was accented by another growl of his stomach, and Lily laughed.

"Yes, it is. Rori and I have been cooking since we got back from the hospital. It's what makes her feel better when she's stressed. She's been through so much, I don't understand why anyone would want to hurt her."

"Well, that's what I plan to find out."

"Actually, no. That's what the Willow Haven Police will find out. Your job is to keep her safe," Steele interjected as they entered the kitchen.

"She must be exhausted, having been through all that. Poor woman."

Lily glanced at him with a surprised expression. "I think you might have the wrong idea about Rori." He didn't think so. Then he came face-to-face with Aurora Prince, and she couldn't have been further from "Betty

Crocker" if she'd tried. Holy shit balls. This was his new assignment?

"Rori, your bodyguard has arrived," Lily said with a laugh and walked around the kitchen island to stand next to her friend. When she lifted her face from whatever she was making, and their eyes met, Raptor grabbed the back of the nearest chair to keep his balance. It was all he could do to keep his jaw from hitting the floor. He'd never ever forget those blue eyes. He'd been searching for her for over two years, and now she was right in front of him.

"I'm Raptor Ramsey, nice to meet you Aurora." He held out his hand, hoping, praying she'd reach for him. The feel of her hand in his would go a long way to convince him that she wasn't a figment of his imagination.

"Please call me, Rori. Only my parents called me Aurora." A shadow passed across her face, but she shook it off and glanced at her hand. After she used the towel to get off the dough, she took his in a firm grip. "I keep telling Lily, I don't need a bodyguard. But she and Alex won't listen."

"I stopped by the bakery and saw the front window. Steele filled me in and there was no way it was an accident. You may not like it, but you're stuck with me for the foreseeable future."

"It was probably just some kids."

"We've been over this. Ethan and Steele don't think so," Lily interrupted. "And the window wasn't the only thing that's happened either. Did they bring you up to speed, Jasper?"

"Yes, ma'am, he did." He still couldn't pull his eyes away from Aurora – Rori. She was even more striking than he remembered. Not beautiful in a traditional sense, and when her wide blue eyes met his he swore she could see into his soul. He hadn't remembered her lush curves or the brown curls that were now tinged with a dusting of flour. He smiled, something he hadn't done a whole lot of lately.

"Jasper?" Lily had still been talking, but he hadn't heard a word she'd said. Could he get away with yes or of course? It probably wouldn't be the wisest course of action since Alex was right there and would report back to Chase.

"I'm sorry. Could you repeat that?"

"No, need," Alex said as he limped into the kitchen. "It's safer to have Raptor on the job than leave you alone over there. Even if you don't think so, we'll all feel better. You'll do it for us, right, Rori?"

Alex was good. From what he already knew of Rori in an emergency, she was too kind-hearted to do anything other than agree. Unless Paris had changed her.

"You guys aren't fair. You do know that, right? I'm a grown woman, have traveled through Europe, and run my own business. I think I can take care of myself."

"But you'll do it for us?"

"Yes," Rori said but exasperation colored her words. Raptor hid his smile. That was his girl. Wait, what? His girl? He'd only just met her, and he'd never been the possessive type. But then Rori was different and he'd never spent two years searching for anyone before.

"I guess you're stuck with me for a bit. Do I call you Raptor or Jasper?"

"Whatever you prefer, ma'am."

"I like Jasper better, you don't look like a bird of prey to me. I hope you don't mind early hours and long days."

"After spending the last ten years in the military, I don't think it will be an issue, ma'am."

"Good to know. Oh and please, stop calling me ma'am. There's really no need, Rori is fine."

"Yes, ma'am...I mean Rori." She hadn't recognized him, but she'd probably tried to put that night out of her mind. But should he tell her who he was? It was probably better to leave it alone, she'd been injured, in shock, and lost her whole family. He would just bring back all the bad memories. Instead, he could start new, and see how they meshed, and see if the feelings he'd tried to suppress for so long were real or just because she'd been the one to get away.

Besides, he had a job to do and it looked like he'd be her protector once again. But this time he'd make sure she stayed safe.

The men who worked for Chase were ex-military, and even though Rori had been impressed by their sheer size, none of them affected her like Jasper. Intense was a good word. Sex god worked too. He'd melt chocolate just from standing next to it. If the heat rising up her neck was any indication, she was ready to melt. What was wrong with her? And why did she get the feeling he was trying to see inside her head?

"You okay?"

"Huh? Oh, yeah. A bit distracted."

Lily laughed and elbowed her in the side. "Really? I couldn't tell."

"Craptastic."

"If I wasn't so fucking head over heels for Alex, I'd be drooling too. But maybe it's just these freaking hormones."

"I'm not drooling." Rori wasn't positive Lily was teasing, and she used the back of her hand to check.

"No, you're not. But you should be."

"Don't be ridiculous. Besides, he's working for me, right? Sort of anyway. And I'm still in mourning."

"Fuck that. It's been more than two years. Jim wouldn't have wanted you to end up a blue-haired old lady baking all day and spending all night alone. Not from what you told me about him."

"True. But..."

"I'm not telling you to jump his bones tonight. Just see where it goes."

"It's not going anywhere. Why would Mr.

sex god want anything to do with me? Have you looked at me lately? I'm sure half the women in Willow Haven follow him around like lost puppies."

"Nope. Alex told me when he's not working he keeps to himself. He doesn't even hang out with the guys. You need to stop hiding behind the fucking counter. I bet you two would be good for each other."

"I don't mean to interrupt, but when's dinner? I'm starving, and Raptor's stomach growled as soon as he walked through the door. Steele has to get back to the station and write up the report."

"Ethan can handle most of it, but he'll be pissed he's missing out on dinner."

"Bull shit. He's practically a chef himself."

"Yeah, but still…"

"We don't need everyone over here tonight. Lily and Rori have been through enough today," Alex said.

"I know. I was going to order pizza but then she started cooking. I'm pregnant, and if you think I'm going to turn down food, you're crazy."

If she hadn't been blushing before, she had

to be three shades of red now. When she glanced sideways at Lily, she was smiling one of her huge, 'oh yeah I'm causing trouble' grins. Great.

"Sorry. It's ready. Let me just put these in the oven, and we can eat." After popping the tray of mini apple strudel in the oven, she and Lily plated the chicken marsala and red potatoes. Lily was right, she couldn't help herself especially when she was stressed. Cooking and baking were about the only things that took her mind off everything else.

With the food set on the table, they sat down to eat. Rori wasn't sure she'd be able to swallow a bite with Jasper's eyes watching her every move. Finally, she couldn't take it anymore. "Is there something wrong? You keep staring at me. You're going to give me a complex."

"I'm sorry. I didn't mean to stare. You weren't what I was expecting."

"It's okay. But…umm…what were you expecting?" Waiting for his answer made her feel like she was back in high school on a first date. The uncomfortable squirmy feeling that made her want to escape. She couldn't remember the last time she'd felt so awkward around a man. But then, she hadn't been around a man since Jim died. Still, there was no reason for it. He wasn't there to date her, only to keep her safe. Even if it was a waste of his time and energy.

"I don't know. I just figured you were older."

"Older?"

"Yeah," Steele interrupted, "I think he thought you were a grandmother type." She'd watched Jasper while Steele spoke, and he looked mortified and pissed at the same time. It eased the squirmy feeling and she struggled not to laugh.

"It's okay. It was probably the name, right? My parents loved the Sleeping Beauty story. When I came along they named me Aurora. But no one calls me that anymore." The relief in his eyes warmed her heart, and she smiled.

"I'm not sure what you call this, but it's delicious. It's been ages since I had a homecooked meal," Raptor commented between mouthfuls. The food was disappearing from his plate in record time and Rori wondered about the last time he'd eaten anything.

"It's one of Rori's recipes. She's a *Cordon Bleu* chef. If you're anything like the rest of Willow

Haven, you'll need to work out more just to keep from gaining weight. I couldn't work there, I'd be enormous."

"Lily's exaggerating but I'm glad you like it. I figured most people eat chicken. I have this horrible habit of cooking or baking when I'm upset or nervous. Usually the women's shelter benefits from it."

"You're going to have a hard time getting rid of me if you cook like this all the time," Jasper said with a wink. Feeling shy as the heat rose up her neck, she looked down at her plate. He was having the strangest effect on her.

"We'll see. Maybe I'll have to start burning things."

"No, you won't," Alex said. "You are too much of a perfectionist in the kitchen."

Their laughter eased the earlier tension, and the conversation turned to food, and what Jasper liked to eat. She couldn't believe he'd been living on mostly food in a pouch for the last decade. Gross. She'd fix that. After four years at the *Cordon Bleu*, Rori was horrified by his description of the MREs. The chefs would have had fits at the mere thought of food in pouches.

After dinner, Steele and Jasper went outside to chat before he headed back to the station.

"What do you think? Will you be okay having him around?"

"Do I have a choice?" Rori had expected to feel awkward about a stranger staying with her in the apartment, but after spending the last few hours with Jasper, she was more comfortable than she'd expected. Except for the whole attraction thing. That could end up being a problem.

"You always have a choice, but I don't think you'll like it."

"I was kind of worried before I met him, but now not so much. Unless he's hiding what he's really like, I think it'll be fine."

"Good. Because there was a Plan B."

"Isn't there always?"

"Yup, sometimes a Plan C too. Actually, there was always a Plan C."

"Out of curiosity, what was Plan B?"

"We'd have you both stay here."

"Yeah, no. That would never work. I start some of the dough at two a.m. Nope. Not happening."

"It wouldn't have been a big deal. I never

sleep through the night anymore. My bladder is controlled by the baby and she doesn't like the idea of me sleeping for more than an hour at a time." Rori laughed and hugged Lily.

"It would be for me. I'd have to get up even earlier to get back into town. Besides, we don't know how long this is going to go on and you're going to have that baby before you know it."

"But it was better than having you freaked out."

"I don't get freaked out." At Lily's look, she amended her last statement. "Okay, so maybe I get a little freaked out. But I'm not the one who thinks someone is out to get me. It's the rest of you."

"C'mon, it's not normal for bricks to go sailing through plate glass windows. And especially not here."

Rori shook her head in frustration as she plated the strudel. Since she'd come back to Willow Haven, she'd caught up with some of her old friends. Anna Taggert had been one of her best friends in high school and if it weren't for her she wouldn't have been able to buy the building and open the bakery. But there were lots of new friends too. Like Lily, Chloe, and

Beth. But when they hovered over her, like now, it drove her a bit crazy. She'd been on her own too long, and it made her feel claustrophobic.

"After dessert, I need to get home. I'm exhausted, and I still have to get Jasper settled." She hadn't heard him and Alex come into the kitchen, and his voice startled her. If it hadn't been for his quick reflexes the plate of strudel would have landed on the floor.

"I didn't mean to scare you."

"It's okay. I'm just not used to people sneaking up on me."

"I'll try to behave, but it's kind of second nature for me after so many years in the military."

"And I'll try not to freak out when you do," Rori said with a smile trying to ease the tension that returned.

Jasper took the plate of pastries and placed them on the island. "How about we take a couple of these for the road."

"It's okay, we can have coffee then leave."

"I didn't realize how early you started until Steele filled me in. You need your rest."

"You don't mind?"

"Of course not. It's my job, remember? To

keep you safe that is." Rori's yawn was the icing on the cake, and there was no changing his mind.

"Okay, you win."

"Here you go," Lily said as she handed Jasper the foil-wrapped package filled with strudel.

"I hope you kept some for you guys?"

"Are you kidding? No way would she give them all away," Alex said with a chuckle. "My wife won't pass up anything that Rori makes."

After saying their goodbyes, they loaded Jasper's gear into the bakery's delivery van.

"I'll stop by tomorrow to see how things are going," Alex said and tilted his chin toward Jasper. Ugh, there was way too much testosterone.

"C'mon, bodyguard, let's get a move on. I have to get up in four hours."

"Yes, boss," Jasper answered with a big grin. He needed to stop looking at her like he wanted to eat her. She'd melt like buttercream if he kept it up. "I can drive."

"It'll be faster for me to do it than have to give you directions."

"I do know my way around Willow Haven. But fine, if you insist."

"I do," Rori said as she climbed into the driver seat. Jasper handed her the seatbelt and then shut her door.

"They sound like a married couple already." Lily giggled. Married? The woman had clearly lost her mind.

"Keep it up, and all the eclairs will be going to Alex."

"Yikes." Lily leaned in the window and whispered, "just give it a chance."

Rori was too tired to argue that this was just a job for Jasper, they'd only met a few hours earlier, and she wasn't on the market anyway. She shouldn't be surprised that Lily was pushing so hard. They'd had this conversation or a variation of it several times over the last six months.

CHAPTER 4

"Are you sure you're not too tired to drive?"

"I'm fine. Seriously. It's not that far to the bakery. I don't sleep all that well anyway." He bet she didn't. She was probably suffering from PTSD and didn't realize it.

"I'm just trying to do my job. You're not going to make this easy, are you?"

"Why do you say that?" Her concentration never deviated from the road, probably trying to avoid looking at him. Seeing him had probably triggered a memory she couldn't quite place.

"Just a feeling. I've survived many missions by trusting my gut."

"Until the last one? The scar on your cheek

doesn't look like it's been there too long, and you're limping."

He was impressed, he barely limped anymore, although the muscles were still weak, but she'd still managed to pick up on it. The scar was an easy guess. It would take another year before it faded enough that it didn't stand out. If she thought that looked fresh, it was good she couldn't see his leg.

"My last mission went to hell before our team realized it. But bad intel is part of the job."

"Do you miss it? Ten years is a long time."

"Yes and no. I miss my team, they were more like family than anything else. And I miss feeling like I'm doing something important. But it was time to move on. Besides my injury, my heart wasn't in it anymore."

"Oh." He'd spent a lot of time reading people, it was part of what had made him good at his job. He knew without a doubt she wanted to ask him why, but she didn't. It was a relief since he wouldn't have known what to tell her. In the last few minutes, he'd already shared more with her than he had with anyone else, even most of his team. He was going to have to watch himself, she was too easy to talk to. He needed to focus. Chase was counting on him, and if Lily and Alex were any indication so was the rest of the town. Maybe once he was assured she was safe, he could see if there was something more between them.

As she parked the van in the spot marked "Reserved for Prince's Patisserie," in the rear lot of the building, his senses were on high alert. There was something off and he learned long ago not to ignore his instincts.

"Why are we here? I thought you didn't have to be at work until two a.m.?"

"I don't but I live upstairs. I bought the building when I decided to open the patisserie. I figured why should I live outside of town when I could live upstairs. It gives me an extra hour of sleep every night."

"Steele conveniently forgot to mention that."

"Don't worry, it's not as small as it looks. It's a three bedroom apartment, so you will have your own space. I know it's kind of awkward but…"

"Hey, don't worry about me. I'm used to sleeping wherever I happen to be—jungle, desert, cave—so no big deal."

"I want to check it out first. Stay here and keep the doors locked." When she didn't answer, he added, "Okay?" This didn't bode well if she was going to fight him every step of the way. How was he supposed to keep her safe?

After an exaggerated sigh, she answered. "Okay. This is the key to the apartment." She handed him her key ring with one key separated out. "It's the door next to the back door of the bakery."

"Got it. Be right back."

Raptor would have preferred to have done this in daylight but surveilling in darkness wasn't a problem. He'd left his pack in the van, but he had his Glock. Armed and ready, he checked out the rest of the parking lot and then approached the door. One key, one lock, no deadbolt. Willow Haven was small but not without crime, and no one thought that she should have a deadbolt at least? It would be the first thing on his list once the hardware store opened. He could have pushed his way in without any effort at all.

A glance toward the van verified that she was still inside. Stepping through the doorway he shouldn't have been surprised it was pitch-black, but he was anyway. He'd expected some light in the hallway. Seriously? She was just asking for trouble. He pulled out the small flashlight he was never without and found the switch, which did jack shit when he flipped it on. Of course. Rolling his eyes for the second time in less than five minutes, he wondered what he'd find at the top of the stairs.

The door didn't have a lock at all. What was wrong with this woman? Tomorrow was going to be a busy day, and if he had to keep an eye on her, he was probably going to have to call in reinforcements.

At least, when he flipped the switch inside her apartment the light came on. It smelled like sugar and cinnamon, and he wondered if it was from the bakery downstairs. Nothing was out of place as he went from room to room, opening all the doors until he was satisfied it was all clear.

He'd just finished his walk through and was in the living room as she stepped into the apartment.

"Is it safe?"

"I thought we agreed you'd stay in the van until I came back and got you."

"We did sort of. I don't like being told what to do and I got tired of waiting. I knew it would be fine."

"Listen, Angel, I know you're not thrilled about having a bodyguard, but you have one. That means you'll listen to me so I can make sure you're safe. Got it?"

Their eyes met and they had their first battle of wills. She blinked first, and he knew he'd won that point. But damn if she hadn't brought his pack in with her.

"Fine. But if I think it's stupid, then I'm going to tell you."

"Alright, I can live with that. But we'll discuss it, and if I have a good reason, you'll follow orders?"

"Orders? I think not." He winced, poor choice of words.

"How about direction?"

"That could work. Now that we got that out of the way let me show you which room is yours. I really am beat and need to get some sleep." He was surprised when she didn't say something about him calling her angel, but maybe she was just too tired to realize.

"Did you lock the downstairs door when you

came in?"

"Yes, do you think I'm stupid?"

"No, but again, it's my job."

Shaking her head, she started down the hallway off the living room. It led to three bedrooms and one bathroom. He'd learned the layout when he did his recon. One bathroom would make life interesting. He hadn't shared with a woman since he'd left home. But other than that, the apartment was a decent size and they shouldn't have trouble staying out of each other's way.

"Here's your room. The bathroom is down the hall next to my room. There are towels on the dresser, and I made up the bed earlier before I went to Lily's. Is there anything else you need? Oh, and if you're hungry help yourself to anything in the kitchen."

"It's great, thank you."

"Okay, sleep well." After a smile that was more like a grimace, she continued down the hall to her room.

"Hey Rori?" She stopped and turned back to look at him.

"Yeah?"

"I'm not trying to give you a hard time, just

keep you safe."

"I understand. It's what everyone thinks and that's the whole problem. I don't need protection. But I guess time will tell."

"Yes, it will."

"I'm sorry to be rude and leave you on your own, but work starts early."

"That's what I've heard. Sleep well, Rori. See you at two."

"Night."

Rori couldn't get to her room fast enough. He was too much. As she leaned against the closed door she thought about him just down the hall. All six foot whatever of solid muscle and it made her lady bits tingle. Can you say muffin man? Or maybe it should be stud muffin man? It took all her willpower to not lean close as she said good night and give him a lick. He smelled like outdoors and citrus…something. She couldn't quite put her finger on it, but she wanted a taste.

Besides waking up feelings that had been dormant for the last couple of years, there was something about him. Something familiar but she didn't know what. Maybe she'd seen him around town. He'd never been in the bakery, that she knew for sure because there was no way in hell or gingerbread that she'd have forgotten that sale.

Exhausted she pulled out her nightgown and brushed her hair before putting it up to wash her face. She'd been trying to focus on the bakery and not all the stuff that had been happening. Keeping most of it to herself, the window had been out of her control, especially with Lily there. Thank God her friend hadn't been seriously injured, or anyone else for that matter. Once Jasper found out about the other stuff she was toast and probably not the French variety with warm maple syrup.

It just seemed like a bit of bad luck at first with the flat tires on the van. The phone calls, the letters, the pictures, but she'd kept that to herself. But the damn plate glass window. And now a new bodyguard who was the best thing since freshly baked bread. But he wasn't there for a relationship, and she wasn't looking for one. Was she even over Jim's death yet? The only thing she'd focused on for the last two years was the bakery. It was her life, her heart, and helped her hold on to the people she'd lost that evening. Her life would never be the same, but she liked to think that they were looking down at her and smiling.

Since coming back to Willow Haven, it had been all about the bakery and closing her parent's house. She still needed to figure out whether to let Anna list it for sale or not. And if not, what was she going to do with it? It was too hard to stay there without them. It made sense to put it on the market. *There, think about that, Rori, instead of the gingerbread man down the hall.*

She changed into her PJs. It was way past her bedtime, and her bed was calling to her. No wonder her mind was scrambled, usually asleep by eight, it was almost eleven. Trying to get through tomorrow was going to be like wading through a tub of molasses.

Throwing her robe on in case she ran into Jasper on the way to brush her teeth, she was thankful two minutes later when she opened the bathroom door and walked in on him.

"Oh my God, I'm so sorry. I should have knocked." Her face burned as she backed up and slammed the door shut.

"It's okay, I'm just brushing my teeth. C'mon in." It didn't seem like such a great idea until he opened the door, and she got a good look at him. With her cheeks already burning, she stared down at his bare feet. From there, her gaze traveled up his jean-clad legs, to the open button at his waist, and up his naked, *oh my God*, chest, and then to his face. His eyes twinkled with laughter as they met hers and he smiled around his toothbrush. She didn't think it was possible, but her face burned even hotter.

"I'm sorry. I'm not used to having anyone else here. It won't happen again."

He spat toothpaste into the sink and rinsed his mouth. "It's okay. We're going to have to get used to each other, it's not a big deal. If I was worried, I'd have locked the door."

Good point. It hadn't been locked, she'd need to remember to do that herself, especially when she was showering. It would be horrible if he walked in when she was naked. Wouldn't it? Damn, girl, brush your teeth and go to bed, you're totally losing it.

"Okay."

"I'm sorry I'm upsetting your routine. I'll leave you to it. Night, Rori."

"Night." She waited until she heard his door close and then brushed her teeth and put on her moisturizer.

Back in her bedroom, she debated whether to lock the door. From the size of his muscles, if he wanted in no lock was going to keep him out, so no on the locked door. She finally climbed into bed and turned out the light and drifted off to sleep with visions of Jasper dancing in her head, which was a nice change from her usual thoughts.

When the alarm went off at one fifteen, she'd have shot it if she owned a gun. With so little sleep, she'd need all the coffee just to pretend to be alive. Add to that her new house-guest/bodyguard, she was going to need a tanker truck full of the caffeinated elixir.

Opening her door, she peered down the hallway and listened to see if Jasper was up yet. When she didn't hear anything, she rushed into the bathroom and locked the door. The hot shower helped to get her blood flowing, but now she needed coffee to complete her morning process. A quadruple espresso sounded about right. She'd forgotten to ask if he drank coffee last night, but she couldn't imagine anyone not imbibing copious amounts of liquid energy in the morning.

Rori was dressed and in the kitchen grinding espresso beans when Jasper appeared by her side freshly showered and smelling delicious. Distracted by his presence, she over ground the beans and had to start over.

"Are you okay?"

"Yeah, just tired and I mutilated the coffee beans."

"I can see that. I was worried you were hoping they were me."

"Uh, no. But that's a thought," she said and turned so he could see her smile. "Do you drink coffee? Espresso?"

"If it's caffeinated I'll drink it."

"A man after my own heart. I usually have coffee up here then make a couple of large coffee urns for the customers when I get downstairs. I think I end up drinking more of it than they do though."

"You'll have plenty of help today," he said with a laugh. The sound poured over her like molasses and warmed her to her core. What was it about this man that he could turn her into mush with just a few words?

CHAPTER 5

After Rori had gone to bed, he'd been unable to resist the call of the apple strudel they'd brought home from Alex's house. If he hadn't already been in awe of her, he would have after his first bite of the flaky pastry melted on his tongue into the perfect combination of sugar and cinnamon covered apples. He'd never been a huge fan of sweets, but she'd changed that. Chase had been right, and he hated to admit it. He totally understood why the people who owned the gym should be thanking her for staying open.

Waking up at zero dark thirty was nothing new to Raptor but heading into the kitchen at that hour for anything other than coffee was something else entirely. After what Steele had said the night before he'd expected the worst, but it wasn't nearly as bad as he'd led him to believe.

From the moment they entered the bakery she was a dynamo of activity. After the fifth time of nearly causing a disaster with a tray of croissants, he stayed out of her way unless she asked for help. While he watched, she turned a bunch of white stuff into assorted breads, rolls, and pastries. It was finally his turn to assist with loading the display cases giving him something more to do than stand guard and drool. His stomach had been growling for hours from the scent of freshly baked bread.

Fifty-pound bags of flour were lined up four high along one wall, and how she lifted them he had no idea. She wasn't a ten-pound weakling but damn those bags were dead weight. The woman was incredible. Next to them were shelves holding large bags of sugar, then rows of spices, yeast, and containers with stuff he'd never heard of before. Who knew there could be so many types of sugar? Rori used at least three different types creating her masterpieces while he tried to stay out of her way. Watching the little powerhouse bake enough to fill the display cases on two hours of sleep and a butt-load of coffee was amazing.

Raptor had never run a business, and after watching all that went into it he was thankful. The bakery was a lot more than just making all the food. Rori had everything timed down to the second as she moved from one project to the next. Always a few minutes ahead of the timer. The dough for the different types of bread and rolls was first so they could rise. Then she'd work on the dough for the croissants that she'd made the day before and get them in the oven.

Once the baking was finished she put in orders for her supplies and had everything done before the bakery opened at six a.m. The last thing she did was make two huge urns of coffee and set them to brew so when she opened the doors everything was ready.

Raptor was surprised to see just how many customers were waiting outside when he unlocked the door. She'd been born and raised in Willow Haven and her parents had been well-known, which probably helped her get started. But this success, it was all on her own with sheer hard work and perseverance. Thinking back to the night they'd met in Paris, he shouldn't have been surprised. She'd been strong then and she was even stronger now. Which made it even harder to believe someone wanted to do her harm.

It was probably a good thing he hadn't been in town much because after that strudel last night he'd be visiting every morning. Since he still wasn't able to go back to his morning ten mile run he'd be in deep shit. He missed it, it had been his routine for over a decade, but he'd been warned that pushing his leg too hard too fast would cause a shitload of other issues. Hopefully, he'd be able to ease into them again as soon as he got clearance from the doc.

It was over an hour before the steady stream of people tapered off long enough for Raptor to be able to grab them each a cup of coffee. "I bet you're ready for a caffeine boost."

"Oh yeah. That's a given and thank you. But I'd really love a nap."

"I can't believe you do all of this yourself every day."

"Why? It's been my dream for as long as I can remember and what I went to school to learn. I enjoy cooking different dishes and creating new recipes, but baking is my first love."

"Lily said you went to the *Cordon Bleu*?"

"Yup. I'd planned on staying in Paris, but then everything changed." This was sticky territory. Did he keep asking questions or should he just admit he was there? In his experience truth was always best. But he didn't want to dredge up the past. Would she even want him around after she knew who he was? It might be too painful, but he didn't want to deceive her either.

"That night was horrific, for sure." She turned to him, her big ocean blue eyes filled with confusion, then recognition dawned as she remembered him. He hadn't been sure she'd seen him clearly enough to recognize his face. Plus the shock of everything she'd been through could have clouded her memories.

"You were there? Yes. You *were* there. Oh my God. It was you. The man who helped me after everything happened. It was *you*, wasn't it?"

"I wasn't sure if you'd remember. I recognized you last night, but when you didn't say anything, I didn't want to push it."

"You saved my life."

"I think the EMTs had more to do with that.

I'm sorry I couldn't help your parents or your boyfriend."

Sadness brought shadows to her eyes, but she didn't let them linger, blinking them away and offering him a bright smile even though it seemed a little forced. "No, don't feel that way. You did so much. I wanted to thank you, but you were gone before I had a chance."

"I was in Paris on a layover on my way back home from a mission. The flight attendant told me about this great restaurant. If I'd been ten minutes earlier things might have been different."

"You can't think like that. I have to believe that everything happens for a reason. If not, then I wouldn't be able to cope with this. I lost everyone I loved in one moment of hatred."

"I'm sorry. Is that why you came back to Willow Haven?" But the jingle of the bell on the door ended their conversation. Relief that she remembered him and didn't blame him for not saving her family, eased the tension in his shoulders. There was so much he wanted to ask about her life since then, but it would have to wait. Maybe knowing he helped her before would make her more accepting of his protection.

Willow Haven was a medium size town, but Jasper would swear that there wasn't a person who lived there that hadn't come into the bakery. Rori had to even bake additional croissants she'd had proofing for tomorrow. He wondered if it was because they'd heard about the window and were there to offer support. But they didn't have another chance to talk until they closed the bakery at three. Alex had come by at lunch and Ethan and Steele had checked on Rori, they said, but he was convinced it was more to check on him. He understood their need to protect her, but she was stronger than they realized, and too stubborn for her own good. As he discovered when he broached the subject of installing the deadbolt locks on her doors.

"It went a lot better than I'd expected today."

"Were you worried about working in a bakery after all of your life and death missions?"

"Maybe a little," Jasper said with a grin. "The closest I get to cooking is throwing something in the microwave."

"Really? That's what you eat when you're

not on a case? Well, while you're here how about I teach you how to cook?"

"You don't have to do that. I've lasted this long I think I'll make it a few years longer. I'm sure the preservatives help keep me young."

Rori choked on her mouthful of coffee, and he had to pound her on the back. "Holy hot buttered biscuits, I can't believe you said that. You're a piece of work, Jasper."

"Yes, I've been told. By you. Several times today as a matter of fact."

"You won't be microwaving any meals in my kitchen, that I can guarantee." Before she finished her sentence she yawned. She had to be running on fumes and needed to get some rest. The plan was a nap for her and some handyman work for him. He was used to functioning on minimal sleep. It was another thing that stayed with him even if he wasn't on the teams anymore.

"I'm going to see if I can have one of the guys come over while I run to the hardware store. You need to get some rest and I need to get the deadbolts for your doors."

"No, you don't."

"Am I your bodyguard? Is it my job to protect you?"

"Yes. But…" He didn't want to argue with her. The bright blue sparks flashing in her eyes was a sure indication she was about to dig her heels in, but this was one she wouldn't win. Still, he needed to diffuse the situation before she got even more riled up. Without thinking about the consequences, he pulled her into his arms and kissed her. He hadn't intended for it to be more than a way to cut off the argument that was coming. But as soon as his lips touched hers it ignited a fire that burned him to his core.

Surprise parted her lips, and he took the opportunity to slide his tongue into her sweet mouth. He couldn't contain his groan as he slid his tongue across hers. She tasted of coffee and innocence. The little voice of reason in his head was yelling at him to stop. It was wrong, he knew it, but he couldn't let go. The more he tasted, the more he wanted. He needed to be inside her, wrapped around her, until there was nothing but the two of them. He struggled with himself to do the right thing and then her arms slid around him. The voice of reason was screaming at him to let her go before he did something stupid. But it didn't feel stupid, or wrong.

Before he could go any further, the phone rang. At first, he didn't realize what it was, but she pulled away as the ringing continued. He groaned but let her go. He'd been saved by the bell—literally.

"I have to get that."

"Right." He wanted to say more but apparently, his brain cells had short-circuited, and he couldn't put two words together. No woman had ever affected him the way Rori did. He envied how poised she was as she answered the phone and took the order. After she hung up, she wrote down some notes in the planner on the counter and then turned to him with an assessing look. Instantly he felt like a twelve-year-old boy who'd been caught smoking behind the school.

"I'm sorry, I shouldn't have done that." At least his brain was putting words together again.

"It probably wasn't the best idea," she said with a smile. "That's cheating if you expect to win all our disagreements that way."

"Were we having a disagreement?" he asked sheepishly.

"We were about to."

"It's not how I remember it." She looked so damn adorable. Jasper dropped a soft kiss on her forehead. "I need to get to the hardware store, and you need to get some rest."

"I still don't think…"

"We had an agreement, didn't we? If I think we need to do something to make sure you're safe, then you'll let me."

"I don't think that's exactly what we agreed on."

"C'mon, Angel, anyone could push in your door before you even knew what was going on. Those locks won't keep anyone out who wants to get in."

"Fine, you win this one. But don't count on winning them all."

"I won't, but I sure as hell liked our discussion." He waggled his eyebrows and laughed when her cheeks turned bright pink. She was sugar and spice and everything nice, just like the nursery rhyme. He couldn't believe women like her still existed in this world. He'd gotten jaded over the years, and she was like a breath of fresh air in a smog-filled world.

"But I'm not napping. I never nap or I won't be able to get to sleep later." He swore she stuck her tongue out at him just before she turned away, and he couldn't wipe the shit-eating grin off his face.

~

"The hardware store is two doors down, why don't you go, and I'll take care of tomorrow's prep work and get everything cleaned up."

"Sorry, no can do. I'm your bodyguard, that means I need to be near the body I'm protecting." She'd known he wouldn't go for it, but she had to try. Her lips still tingled from his kiss, and how she'd just melted in his arms. She needed some space from Mr. Stud Muffin to process the feelings churning in her head.

The kiss was a surprise, she should have pushed him away, but instead, she'd pulled him closer. Thank God the phone rang, if not who knows what would have happened next. It's not like she had been ready to stop him. Her mind was like scrambled eggs around him. She'd loved Jim and planned to spend the rest of her life with him, but his kisses never left her craving more and a flash of guilt soured the coffee she'd drank.

A job, that's all she was to him, and she needed to remember it. No more kisses, no more betraying Jim's memory. He'd loved her, proposed to her, and she still had his ring tucked away in the box in her dresser. Every so often she'd slide it on her finger and for a few minutes pretend that November fifteenth had never happened. Pretend that her life hadn't changed forever.

Guilt wasn't doing her any favors, and as Anna was fond of reminding her, Jim wouldn't have wanted her to spend the rest of her life mourning him. It was on her. She made herself feel the guilt, stuck in the molasses of life, instead of pushing ahead. Still, she was living her dream—mostly. Close enough. The bakery brought her joy and kept her sane. It was enough. Or it had been until Jasper walked back into her life.

"C'mon, slowpoke. It won't take long, and then I'll help you get ready for tomorrow."

"Okay. Let me grab my purse from upstairs."

"You don't need it."

"Seriously? Are we going to argue over everything? My doors, my locks, my money." This was one thing she refused to back down on. She had the money and could take care of herself.

"Okay, Angel, if that's what you want, then let's get a move on. You need to get back into your routine, so you're not dragging your honey buns around tomorrow."

Did he just call her butt honey buns? No way. She was about to cover him in flour when she saw the huge grin on his face. Teasing was okay and a heck of a lot easier on her heart than kissing.

Without thinking, she'd headed out the back door of the bakery without waiting for him. Still dazed from his kisses, she didn't notice the painting on the outside door to her apartment until she started to slide the key in the lock. Startled, she shrieked and stared in horror at her door. Jasper was at her side before the sound of her scream faded from her lips. He pushed her behind him, ensuring she was protected.

Someone had painted the word *WHORE* across her door in bright red. They'd even sprayed the doorknob. There was so much paint it dripped down her door and onto the pavement and it looked like a pool of blood. No way was this a prank by teenagers. As much as she hated to admit it, someone had it out for her.

"Did you touch the door?"

"No, I was about to slide my key into the lock when I saw it."

"Good. Don't touch anything, I'm going to call Steele."

"Really? Do we have to call him? Can't we just get paint and cover it? We're going to the hardware store anyway."

"Rori, every incident needs to be reported. You have been doing it all along, right?" He wasn't going to like her answer, she knew it, and he could probably read it all over her face. She was never good at hiding her feelings.

"Well…umm…not exactly. The flat tires and broken window, yes. I put in an insurance claim, and they needed the police reports."

"There's more than that? Did you tell Lily, Alex, anyone?"

"Nope, like I said, I thought it was just a bunch of teenagers blowing off steam. Alex and Lily didn't agree, and neither did anyone else apparently. That's why you're here. But no, they don't know about the other stuff. None of it was a big deal. It could have just been bad luck that happens to everyone."

"You and I are going to have a long discussion later after we finish with Steele and I change the locks. Hopefully, the door is the extent of the damage."

For the first time, Rori was afraid. If everyone was right, then someone was trying to make her life miserable or worse. She knew most of the people in town and she couldn't imagine it was one of them. Who could it be?

CHAPTER 6

Before they'd gone back to the station, Ethan, Steele, and Jasper checked out her apartment, thankfully nothing had been out of place. He'd be lying if he didn't admit he was relieved it hadn't been touched. Hearing her scream was like a knife to his heart and he couldn't get to her fast enough. That she'd gone outside without him was a whole other issue that he was going to have to discuss with her. But that instant when he didn't know if she was okay had been terrifying. Once he realized she was fine, his anger blossomed. Rori wasn't one of those too stupid to live women, but she sure as hell was stubborn. He had a horrible feeling he'd be furious by the time she told him everything that had been going on. It had to stop, the fucker needed to be caught. If he was lucky, he'd be the one to catch the guy, and he'd make sure it was the last time he harassed anyone ever again.

As soon as Ethan and Steele headed back to the station to file the report, they went to the hardware store. The original plan had been for a couple of deadbolts and lightbulbs for the hallway, but the list now included paint to cover the back door and add motion-activated flood light for the back of the building. He wasn't taking any more chances. What bothered him most was the fear on Rori's face. It tore him up, and he was in full on protection mode. Only years of training had stopped him from pulling her into his arms and promising her that everything would be okay. But until he figured out who was harassing her and why, he couldn't make that promise.

After they returned from the hardware store, Jasper got to work. He wasn't a regular handyman, but he'd been around enough tools in his life to take care of this type of stuff. He'd rechecked the apartment to make sure it was still safe and left Rori upstairs to relax.

"I have to do tomorrow's prep."

"Relax for a bit, let me get this stuff done then I'll help you. Deal?" It was obvious she wanted to argue, but from the huge dark circles under the deep blue eyes, she was just too tired and freaked out to push it.

"Fine. I'll see what I can come up with for dinner."

"Is there a restaurant we can go to instead? I think you've been through enough today."

"The diner…"

"Perfect."

"But…"

Jasper didn't even say anything, just gave her the *look* he'd used on his team members, it never failed to silence any opposition, and it was no different with Rori. His poor angel had been through the wringer.

"Come and get me when you're done."

Nodding, he went to work after watching her walk up the stairs to the apartment. Damn she had a fine butt, he'd been teasing her with the honey buns remark, but he'd bet it was the truth. She'd been so soft against his hard body and had curves in all the right places.

He'd felt the presence behind him, and pulled his gun and turned in one liquid motion.

"Hey, easy, bro. I'm a friendly." Chase backed up with his hands in the air. It took Jasper a second or two to stand down, his senses on high alert.

"Sorry. You should know better than to sneak up on me."

"I do, but I figured you heard me."

"I did. But I didn't know it was you. And after this…" Jasper stepped away from the door to show Chase the damage. "I wasn't taking any chances."

"Can't say that I blame you. The town is all abuzz about the, and I quote 'sexy guy working with Rori.' Everywhere I went today I heard the whispers. Then when Steele called to tell me what happened, I wanted to check on Rori."

"Don't you mean 'check' on me?"

"No, I meant Rori. If I didn't think you could do this job, I wouldn't have given it to you."

Jasper swallowed his next words and took a deep breath. "Thanks, boss. I really won't let you down."

"I know. Steele also told me that she's the

girl you've been trying to find for the last two years. Is that true?"

It didn't pay to lie, he knew he'd find out the truth anyway, but how Steele had known he'd love to find out. "Yes, it's true. But it doesn't change anything. And before you ask, yes, I told her who I am."

"Good. I wouldn't have expected any different. But you're the talk of the town apparently. The blue hair brigade has gone on high alert."

"Blue hair brigade? What the fuck are you talking about?"

"The elderly women in town, nothing gets by them. Surely, you noticed a bunch of the women in the bakery today."

"Not really. I was focusing more on the males who came in. But maybe I did see a couple of older women. I couldn't believe the amount of business she does."

"I warned you. She found a niche that needed to be filled. Since everyone knew her or her family they were more than happy to support her. But that also makes it worse that someone is gunning for her."

"I know. I don't get it either and she can't think of anyone who would want to hurt her.

After it went so well in the bakery, in other words, no trouble with broken windows or anything, I was surprised to see this out here. It makes me wonder if it's the same person. The window was so blatant, but this is hidden behind the building. Not many people would see it. It's definitely a more personal attack."

"Agreed. How is Rori holding up?"

"She's shaken up. Scared but working hard to hide it. Apparently, there have been other issues besides what she told Lily about, and now this today. You were right to suggest a bodyguard. I don't have a good feeling about this."

"Let me know if you need backup. Any of the guys at ESP will be happy to help out."

"Thanks, I'll keep you updated. I'm gonna give Alex a call later and see if he can do some digging, maybe his computer geekery will turn up something."

"Good, I'll give Ethan a call and have him talk to Anna. She and Rori were best friends in high school. Maybe she'll remember someone who wasn't a fan. She was always so quiet I can't imagine it though."

"Quiet? She sure as hell changed then, she's one bossy woman now." He'd heard her come down the stairs and figured a little provocation wouldn't hurt. He enjoyed making her eyes flash, and her cheeks turn shades of pink. Who was he kidding, he couldn't get enough of any part of her.

"I heard that."

"What are you doing down here? You're supposed to be resting."

"I was hoping you'd be done. There's a lot of prep to do for tomorrow still. And like you said I need my rest later."

"It's only been ten minutes, Angel."

Chase laughed and raised an eyebrow, probably at his use of his nickname for Rori. But Jasper rolled his eyes. "I can stay with her in the bakery while you take care of what you have to."

"You've got time for that?"

"Yeah."

"Thank you so much. I really need to get that croissant dough prepped, or there won't be any for tomorrow."

"Oh hell. We can't have that. Willow Haven would be in an uproar."

"There are a few leftover eclairs if you're hungry."

"Oh yeah, but only if you promise not to tell Faith. She'll make me do an extra hour on the treadmill. I want to shoot that damn thing."

"I'll take one of those too if you're offering."

"Nope, none for you. Don't you have work to do?" She'd told him, and he howled with laughter as Chase followed her into the bakery. She was everything he'd imagined and more. As much as he wanted to get to the bottom of this, he hoped that she wouldn't push him away when it was over.

For now, he needed to get his "chores" done so he could take his stubborn angel to dinner.

"Y ou two getting along okay?"

Rori gave Chase an assessing look. If it were Lily or Anna, she'd come clean about her feelings, but no way was she going there with Chase. She'd known him a long time and really liked his fiancé, Faith, but he was also Jasper's boss. "Yeah, for the most part. When he's not being a stubborn pig-headed man."

"You mean like all of us?" He was right, Anna complained about the same thing with

Ethan and Rori laughed, really laughed for the first time in a while. That's when she realized how worried she'd been about everything. Today, except for being exhausted from lack of sleep, had been a good day, and fun with Jasper, until they'd found the mess on her door.

"I guess so. But did you have to find the worst of the worst for my bodyguard?"

"Hey, he was available. You have to take what you can get," Chase said with a laugh. "Now how about one of those eclairs?"

"You got it, and I'll pack up a couple for you to take home to Faith."

"I have to share? That's just not right."

Rori turned to answer and laughed when she saw his chocolate mustache. "Don't even go there. Not if you know what's good for you. And if you don't wipe your face, she's sure to figure it out anyway."

"It's your fault."

"You can keep telling yourself that, but I just create them, I don't force anyone to eat them." Only half kidding, she appreciated how each of them had gone out of their way to help her little bakery become a success. It could have just as easily flopped big time. She sold treats not necessities, and you could get the same thing in the grocery store, well not exactly the same. She took pride in everything she made, nothing was mass produced. Too bad there was that one person who had to make problems, at least she hoped it was only one.

Not knowing how long she had before Jasper would be done, she grabbed the croissant dough from the fridge and began rolling it out on the steel surface. It was a tedious task, but one she enjoyed. In her classes at the *Cordon Bleu*, she'd worked hard to be the best, make the lightest dough, the creamiest custards, richest fondant, and she'd usually succeeded. It had caused some issues with some of her classmates, but she never let it bother her. She'd forgotten about most of that, it seemed like a lifetime ago. But could it be one of them? It seemed unlikely, why would they come all this way to cause her trouble? Nope, it had to be someone local.

The croissants were ready for baking and she put them back in the refrigerator to set for the night. Stepping back and admiring the trays of pastries like an artist admiring a painting, she smiled then yawned.

Gathering the empty containers, trays, and

mixing bowls, she dumped them into the sink. It was then she realized Chase was on his cell phone. Was she so tired she hadn't heard it ring? Rather than make noise with the dishes, she went into the front of the bakery to give him some privacy.

Grabbing one of her signature pink and black boxes, she picked out some petit fours to bring upstairs for dessert later. She planned on convincing Jasper that it would be easier to stay in tonight. The last thing she wanted to do was go to the diner, especially after this afternoon's discovery. It could be any of the townspeople, and the thought that it could be anyone freaked her out.

"What do you think you're doing?"

Rori jumped and almost dropped the box of pastries. "Do you always have to sneak up on me?"

"Don't turn this on me, Angel. You were supposed to stay with Chase, and I find you alone out here."

"C'mon, you can't be serious. He's just in the kitchen."

"And anyone could have grabbed you without him realizing."

"Does this mean you're going to follow me into the bathroom now too?"

"Hmmm, maybe the shower," Jasper said as he waggled his eyebrows, and she worked hard to hold back the giggle. When he did that thing with his eyebrows, it made her laugh but it also accentuated his scar. She'd had to stop herself a few times from asking if it was from the night he'd rescued her, but it looked more recent. It wouldn't be polite to ask, but she wondered just the same.

"You're terrible."

"No, Angel, I'm very, very good." Now he did it, her cheeks had to be flaming, and they weren't the only thing getting hot.

Before she could think of a suitable answer, Chase joined them.

"I'm sorry. I have to go, problems with another case. Are you all set, Jasper?"

"Yup, thanks for helping out."

"No problem. Let me know if there are any new developments."

"Don't forget the box of eclairs," Rori reminded him.

"As if. Jasper, call if you need anything."

"Will do, boss." Chase and Jasper

exchanged looks before he left through the kitchen. She was dying to ask what that was about but figured she might not want to know.

"Do you want to inspect my handy work?"

"Can I finish washing up first?"

"Is that all that's left to do?"

"Yup. Then I'm done for the day."

"Good. I'll help."

While they cleaned the counters and washed the dishes, he asked about the bakery and how she decided what she'd make, it was a nice break from the teasing. But it did keep her a bit off balance. If he was only toying with her, she wasn't sure her heart could handle it.

He was a professional and she was sure that sleeping with a client was off limits. After two years of celibacy, the kiss had ignited a fire she'd forgotten existed. It had to be the reason she was twisted in a pretzel and wanted to jump him. Either way, she needed to get herself under control, sleeping with her bodyguard was one cliché she didn't plan to experience, maybe.

CHAPTER 7

Could she really be as innocent as she seemed? The slightest teasing turned her cheeks the most amazing shade of pink. It was becoming his favorite color, and he had to fight the desire to slide her clothing off and see if it tinged her whole body. Chase would probably kill him, Alex, too. Hell, there'd be a line outside with one of those take a number machines. Since he'd royally screwed up the last assignment when he'd decked the client, it wouldn't be a good idea to sleep with this one. But trying to explain that to his body was another story. The words *mine* kept echoing in his head whenever he got near her.

If he wasn't in love with her, he was damn close, especially if walking around with a perpetual hard-on was any indication. It hadn't been twenty-four hours since his eyes met her's at Alex's house and he'd been rock hard almost the entire time. His set of blue balls was going to be worthy of the *Guinness Book of World Records* if he didn't get some relief soon.

Over the last two years, he'd turned her into the perfect woman. One that couldn't possibly be real. Yet the more he was around her, the more he realized he'd been spot on. Everything this world tried to destroy was in abundance in his angel.

As she washed, he dried, and they made quick work of the cleanup. Then his stomach grumbled. Neither of them had eaten since they'd grabbed a croissant and coffee during a mid-morning break and that was hours ago.

"Where's the diner? Is it close enough to walk there?" He'd lived in Willow Haven for about four months but if he'd spent a week there between missions it had been a lot. But he needed some space between him and Rori. Sitting in the truck was too close, too tempting to pull her into his arms again.

"We could walk, but I could throw something together just as quickly as it would take to get there and order."

"Are you embarrassed to be seen with me? I know I'm not the prettiest guy around…"

"Are you kidding me? You're gorgeous." He knew the exact moment when she realized what she'd said because her cheeks turned a deep shade of magenta. Yup, it was definitely his new favorite color.

"I'm glad you think so. But I usually scare small children everywhere I go."

"No, you don't. You're just messing with me. I don't believe it."

"I do. Sometimes, anyway. But if it's not me, why don't you want to go out? If the bags under your eyes are any indication you're practically dead on your feet. Won't it be easier to let someone else cook for you?"

"I am tired. I'm not going to lie, but after the door thing, I'm kind of freaked out. It could be anyone here. People I see every day. I won't be able to eat if I'm looking around wondering who hates me so much that they'd put that word on my door."

It made sense, and even though he got it, it

pissed him off that she was too scared to go out. That's why he was there, to protect her, to keep her safe. But if she wanted to stay home then so be it. After years of MREs, he could live on PB&J and be happier than a pig in shit. Besides, there were still a few apple strudels left from last night.

"We'll catch this asshole, and then you'll be able to go out without worrying, I promise."

"Thanks. I guess I owe Chase extra treats for sending you to protect me."

"From what he said, he'd definitely take it as payment. I never had much of a sweet tooth but you've made me a convert too." He couldn't resist giving her a wicked grin. He was starving and not just for food, his mouth was watering for another taste of her, she smelled like the bakery, sweet.

As she walked past him she punched him in the arm. Okay, not just sweet, his angel had a feisty center. She double checked the lock on the bakery door and then turned to survey his handiwork on the apartment entrance.

"Wow, I can't even tell it was there. It's great. Thank you so much. You even got the paint off the doorknob."

"Yup, a little paint stripper. I was happy to see it didn't destroy the knob. There are two sets of keys to the new deadbolts. I left yours on the table upstairs. I'll keep the second set until we figure out who is behind this crap."

"That's fine, it'll make it easier if you're not ready when I leave for the bakery in the morning."

"No, it won't because that's not happening." He gently grasped her shoulders and turned her body so she could see the new floodlight. As soon as his fingers made contact with her, a burning desire ignited within him. Unable to resist, he leaned down and kissed the side of her neck. It had to be safer than her lips, or he thought so until he inhaled her scent.

It hadn't been a one time deal, she smelled like vanilla and cinnamon sugar and felt like heaven in his arms. Turning her toward him, his lips traveled across her jaw to her lips. Pulling her even closer, she'd feel his erection, but he didn't care. Groaning as her belly leaned against his rock hard dick, he worried he'd lose it right there.

Somehow sanity returned. He was pawing her like a high school kid outside in the parking lot where anyone could see them, could hurt her. As he broke the kiss, she looked at him with confusion and longing in her eyes. A glimmer of hope filled his heart that she wanted him as much as he needed her.

"I think we should continue this upstairs, where we are alone." He might as well have poured cold water over her head or flipped a switch. One second she was oozing lust and the next she closed up like a bank vault.

"I'm sorry…"

"No, don't be. I don't know what I was thinking. No wait, that's the problem. As soon as you touch me, I can't think."

"Is that a bad thing?"

"Isn't it? My place is here. But once you've caught this guy you'll be off on your next assignment. I don't do casual relationships."

"It doesn't have to be that way." She didn't look convinced, and how could he blame her? She hadn't remembered him until yesterday and had no idea he'd been trying to find her for what felt like a lifetime.

∽

What the heck was she thinking? He was there for a job, and a job only. If she didn't start remembering that, she was going to be in a world of pain when he left. And what would keep him in the small town when he'd traveled the world and probably been with tons of beautiful women? It's not like she was a catch. She looked in the mirror every day and saw herself. What did they call women like her? Fluffy? Curvy? Whatever, she didn't care. Then there was her baggage. It had been over two years and she still had terror-filled nightmares about the attack in Paris.

But Jasper, damn. Her heart wanted to tell her brain to take a hike. The scar on his face made him even sexier. He'd earned that fighting for their country to keep them free. It might as well have been a medal of honor. Would giving in to her desires be so bad? At least, after he was gone, she'd have the memories.

"Rori? Are you okay?"

"Yes, sorry. What else did you want to show me?" He looked perplexed at her attitude change. Well, join the club. It was too much too fast. She needed to put some space between them so she could think because she sure as hell couldn't when he was close enough to lick.

"I installed a floodlight with a motion sensor. Now when anything moves back here, the light will come on."

"Thank you. It'll make it so much better when it's dark out here."

"I'm surprised you didn't put one up when you opened the bakery since you're at work in the middle of the night. It's not safe in the dark. Anyway, let's go upstairs, I fixed the light in the hallway too. Now you can see when you're going up the stairs."

"I should have changed those bulbs. I kept thinking about it but never got around to buying the new ones."

"You're all set now," he said with a smile. When he smiled his eyes crinkled up at the corners, and it softened the hard edges of his face. His eyes held a lot of pain, he'd seen too much suffering. Could she be the one to make the pain disappear? Ugh, there she was going on again.

"Is this normal bodyguard stuff? I mean, fixing lights, changing locks? It doesn't seem like that would be part of the normal job description."

"It's not. Or hasn't been before now but I didn't mind. I like working with my hands, and it's to keep you safe. And that is my job. I'll do whatever it takes."

"Right. It's the job." He frowned but didn't say anything, just held the door open for her to go inside. He'd done a good job, whatever type of light bulbs he'd put in were really bright, and not even a shadow lurked as she climbed the stairs to her apartment. At the top of the stairs, he unlocked the new deadbolt and opened the door.

Everything was the same as they'd left it early that morning. Relief washed over her that whoever had painted downstairs hadn't gotten inside and destroyed her home.

"If you promise to stay put, I'll grab a quick shower and then help with dinner."

"I won't go anywhere, I promise. Enjoy your shower." With a short nod, he headed to his room.

Taking a deep breath, she rotated her shoulders to try to relax the aching muscles. It was the same every day. By the time she was done her body ached and she usually took a shower before fixing something for dinner. But she'd gladly give up dibs on the first shower to have some alone time.

In the kitchen, she opened the refrigerator and surveyed the contents. There wasn't a whole lot of anything, but that didn't mean she couldn't whip up something. Simple would be the word of the evening. Grilled cheese was tempting, but it probably wouldn't be enough food for Jasper. Instead, she whipped up a quiche. Grabbing the eggs, heavy cream, Swiss cheese, bacon, a tomato, and onion she set them on the counter. Then took out one of the piecrusts she'd made over the weekend. Cooking the bacon first, she chopped the vegetables. After the bacon was done, she sauteed the veggies in the grease and then added everything to the egg and cream mixture, salt, pepper, basil and a bit of garlic powder and it was done.

As she slid the quiche into the oven, she heard his footsteps in the hallway. Too bad the man didn't take long showers. Cooking always helped her settle herself, and she mentally crossed her fingers that she had found some inner calm. Not realizing he was right behind her, she backed into him as she stood up after she closed the oven door.

"Damn. You smell good." So much for thinking she'd gotten herself under control.

"I'm glad you think so. What can I do to help? I thought I smelled bacon when I was getting dressed."

"You did. I made a quiche. It'll take a bit to bake, but while we're waiting I'll make a salad. Easy peasy."

"Quiche? What's that?"

"I guess it's sort of like an egg pie with stuff in it. Or maybe an omelet in a pie crust."

"Really? That sounds kind of weird. Egg pie? But if it has bacon in it, it's got to be good. Why don't you go shower? I can make a salad. I know how to do that."

"Are you sure?"

"Yup. Then we can have dinner and talk until bedtime. When do I have to take the egg pie out of the oven?"

"It bakes for almost an hour. It'll be fine, I'll check it after my shower."

"Great. Go, angel, you're dead on your feet."

"I'm fine. Used to this, really. I won't be long."

"Take as long as you like, I'll be right here."

CHAPTER 8

As she opened the bathroom door his scent washed over her, and she groaned. It was like walking into a steamy hug. On unsteady legs, she slid out of her clothes and turned on the water. Tired or turned on, she wasn't sure which was taking more of a toll on her composure. Either way, she needed to get a grip.

A glance in the mirror explained why he thought she was exhausted. The dark circles under her eyes and her pale cheeks made her look like one of the walking dead. The stress was catching up to her. Why couldn't the world just leave her alone for a while? She'd paid enough of a price.

When she came back to Florida, Willow Haven, she'd started over, modified her plan and opened the bakery. She enjoyed running the little shop. It was close to what she'd dreamed about when she was a child, and then a teen. She still remembered how ecstatic she was when she got the acceptance to the *Cordon Bleu*. It was as close as she'd get now. The rest of the dream, to open her bakery in Paris and live happily ever after, that part was long gone. Left to bleed out on a corner in the city she'd idolized.

There had been so many plans made for the future, for her and Jim. Her parents were going to help her open the bakery. They had a little apartment close to the magazine where Jim worked, and she hoped to find space for the bakery near there. The competition would have been fierce, but she'd loved Paris. But all it took was a few bullets and lots of hate to change it all. She'd never forget gazing into her parents' unseeing eyes.

As the hot water sluiced over her tense muscles, tears rolled down her cheeks. It was the only place she'd allow herself to cry. The water washed away the tears as quickly as they fell. She'd shed countless tears, for days—months—

afterward. During her hospital stay as she healed from her wounds. She'd sunk into a deep depression. One she hadn't been sure she wanted to escape. It would have been easier to end it than go on alone. The counselors had helped, and she'd recovered, at least on the outside.

The trip home with the two caskets had been devastating. Jim's family had insisted he be buried in their family plot in Boston, and they'd taken his body while she was still in the hospital. She'd never met them, and they hadn't stopped by when they collected his body. It was strange. It didn't make sense that they wouldn't have wanted to meet his fiancé even if they weren't going to be married. But he'd told her that he'd had a falling out with them. His father had wanted him to be a lawyer, join his firm. The family was old money and all the men followed that path. But Jim wanted to follow his own dream and they hadn't forgiven him before he'd died.

She hadn't fallen apart like this in a while, but she'd been terrified when she'd seen the door. It was too much. But it was time to move on. Maybe a fling with Jasper was just the thing she needed to push her out of her comfort zone. She'd been so engrossed in her thoughts, she never heard him knock on the door.

"Are you okay? Rori? Answer me."

"Oh. Yes, I'm fine. Sorry. Don't come in." Mortified that he might see her naked body, she didn't know what to cover first with her hands. If anyone had been watching, they would have laughed. "Did you need something?"

"No, I just wanted to make sure you were alright." He'd opened the door and was standing in the doorway.

"I'm fine. I promise. I'm just enjoying the heat of the water. I'll be out shortly so you can leave now."

"You sure you don't want some company?" Oh, did she ever. But no way. She was still deciding if this was the path she would travel, and the last thing she wanted was the first view of her body to be in the bright bathroom light. Candlelight would be so much better, or darkness... that would work.

"No, I think I'm fine by myself. Could you shut the door you're letting the cold air in?" He wasn't really, but she needed him to leave before she accepted his offer.

Hearing his chuckling as he closed the door didn't help anything. But hearing the decisive click when it closed made her sink against the tiled wall and breathe a sigh of relief. Hornier than a teenager, she needed to stop this flip-flopping around like a crazy woman. It was time to shit or get off the pot as her mom used to say. Mom would have liked Jasper, and probably her dad too. Or at least he would have won him over eventually. Shaking her head, she finished rinsing the soap off and climbed out of the shower.

She'd totally forgotten to bring fresh clothes into the bathroom. It wasn't her usual routine since she lived alone. It didn't matter if she walked around in a towel. But it mattered today. Ready to kick herself, she pulled open the door enough to peek out and see if he was around. When the coast looked clear, she ran to her room and closed and locked the door. Then she leaned against it like she'd been running for her life. What the heck was she doing? Laughing until tears poured down her cheeks, she couldn't believe she just did that. She was thirty-one years old, and definitely not a virgin, so why was she fighting the attraction so hard? And why was she running to her bedroom to hide like a fifteen-year-old?

"Everything okay in there?" His knock made her laugh even harder.

"Yeah, everything's fine. I'll be right out," she said while trying to catch her breath.

"Are you sure? You sound kind of hysterical in there."

"Yup, it's all good. Go check on that salad, it might be wilting."

"Okay good idea." As he walked away, she snorted. It was the first thing she could think of to tell him to do. Check on the salad, seriously? And he did it? Wow. He really did need help with this kitchen skills.

Pulling herself together, she grabbed a pair of yoga pants and an oversized t-shirt, then pulled her thick curls into a messy bun. Keeping it up was a lot easier to deal with, and a necessity in the bakery, even if it wasn't her most attractive look. Chewing her lip, she considered getting out her blow dryer and adding a little makeup. But hearing his footsteps in the hallway killed that idea. What was he doing? Patrolling the hallway to keep her safe? Giggling again, she pulled open the bedroom door and almost walked headfirst into a wall of chest.

"You do know it's only the two of us here, right? I don't think you need to be on guard."

"I wasn't exactly patrolling."

"No? You checked on me a couple of times in less than a half hour. Unless I'm mistaken, you were about to do it again." Looking sheepish, he smiled.

"You've been through hell for the last few days. Give a guy a break for wanting to make sure you're okay." Well, when he put it that way she felt bad for saying anything.

"You do know I've managed to take care of myself for most of the last thirty-one years, right?"

"You're that old?" He said what? Oh no he didn't.

"Did you just say I'm old? Because if you did you'd better remember to lock your door tonight or you might find yourself knocked over the head with my cast iron skillet."

"I didn't mean it like that."

"No? Why don't you try to dig yourself out of that hole, and I'll check on the quiche?" Following a few steps behind her, she could almost feel the wheels in his brain turning as he tried to figure out what to say next. She wasn't mad. It was funny, and she'd been trying to hold in her laughter. It was a nice change that she wasn't the one squirming about what to say.

The quiche wasn't quite done yet. Even her stomach was growling now. But you can't rush perfection. Checking on the salad, she was impressed with his prep skills. Maybe there was hope for him yet. "Nice job with the veggies."

"I tried, I figured you'd want everything bite size, so I had to cut them down a bit."

She smiled as she checked the full salad bowl. He'd chopped everything into one inch size pieces. It surprised her that he'd put thought into the chore. The rare instances she'd convinced Jim to help, he'd do just enough to finish whatever she'd asked without caring how it turned out. Most of the time she'd have to go back and fix whatever he'd done.

"Good to know we don't have to start with Salad 101 and can progress right to cooking eggs."

"What? I thought you were kidding about the cooking lessons."

"Nope. Everyone should know how to cook the basics at least."

"I don't need to. I'm hardly ever home and when I am the last thing I want to do is spend time in the kitchen. I'd rather grab a beer and watch whatever game is in season." That didn't surprise her, but she wasn't going to back down. Although, if she was trying to keep him at arm's length, teaching him to cook and bake wasn't the way to do it.

"How much longer 'til that egg pie thingy is done? I'm starving."

"Quiche, it's called quiche. Not long, but we can eat the salad now instead of waiting. Do you want a beer with dinner?"

"Are you going to have one?"

"I'm not a big beer fan, I usually keep it here for guests. I prefer wine."

"Do you have a lot of guests?"

"No, not that it's any business of yours." Damn, she'd gone and done it. Got him riled up again. Just when she thought they'd have a peaceful meal and he'd forget about the conversation he'd promised they'd have.

When he didn't say anything, she grabbed the bottle of Pinot Grigio out of the refrigerator and reached for a glass. Waiting for his next question or answer about the beer, he surprised her when he spoke.

"I'll have wine, too."

Raising her eyebrows, she grabbed another wine glass from the cabinet. Then carried the bottle and glasses over to the small dining room table. It would be the first meal she'd shared with anyone since she moved in. It was kind of nice. Who was she kidding? Having him around was wonderful and exasperating at the same time.

He picked up the salad bowl and followed her to the table. "You know, I didn't mean you were old. It just came out wrong. I thought you were barely into your twenties. You look so young."

"Nice try."

"Seriously, Angel. I figured you were way too young for me." Jasper grabbed her hands and stopped her from heading back to the kitchen. Tilting her chin, she had no choice but to look into his hazel eyes. "You're beautiful, amazing, and in case I haven't made it abundantly clear already, I really want you."

"You want me?" her voice came out in a

high squeak. He grinned, but the intensity in his eyes raised goosebumps on her arms and sent a shiver of longing along her nerve endings.

"Yes, Angel. For as long as I can have you. I know I should wait until you're not my client, but I've been searching for you for so long. I'd almost convinced myself you weren't real. And then there you were in front of me. The woman who'd eluded me for two long years."

"You've been searching for me?" Her brain couldn't put more than two words together. She sounded like a nitwit.

"Yes, I have. I'll explain everything if you let me. Just know that I'm serious, I want to make love to you. I will wait until you're ready but don't doubt for a minute that I want to make you mine."

She was sure she was impersonating a fish. Her mouth opened and closed while she tried to come up with something to say. He saved her. Before she could find her words, his lips took hers, his tongue demanding entrance to her mouth. He crushed her against him leaving her no doubt that he'd meant what he said. The erection pushing against her belly was all the proof she needed. His passionate kisses made her knees weak, and she grabbed his waist to keep from falling.

If he didn't stop now, he'd carry her down the hall to her room. As much as it killed him to release her, he had no choice. He'd made her a promise he intended to keep. She would be the one to set the pace no matter how much it killed him. With a groan that echoed through his body, he released her and took a step back.

"I'm sorry. That wasn't fair, I just finished telling you I'd give you time."

"It…it's okay, really. I just…"

"I think the egg pie might be burning." Apparently, you can take the man out of the military but not the military out of the man, he'd always be aware of his environment.

"What?"

"Dinner?"

"Oh no." Rori ran into the kitchen and opened the stove. He looked over her shoulder as she pulled it out of the oven.

"It doesn't look too bad."

She gave him a 'you've got to be kidding'

look while shaking her head. "Damn. I don't remember burning anything since I was ten."

"I bet we can cut off the crispy edges and it'll be fine."

"It's egg-based, it will have absorbed the burnt flavor."

"How about we give it a try? I'm game if you are?" She didn't look convinced, but in the end, their hunger won out and his libido cooled off. It was okay though, he needed to talk to her, lay the ground rules and make sure she understood it could be a matter of life or death if she didn't follow them.

CHAPTER 9

"This is pretty good."

"Quiche. It's not a hard word."

"It's weird though. Didn't there used to be a thing about real men not eating it?"

"Yes, but you're eating it, and if what happened earlier was any indication, you are definitely a real man." In his head, he did a fist pump, maybe the mood wasn't completely lost. They still needed to have the talk about all the issues she'd been having and following his rules. It sucked that he wasn't any closer to any answers. Chase sent him a text while she was in the shower to let them know that Ethan and Steele hadn't been able to identify the fingerprints. With no help there, they were still at square one.

"Well, it's good."

"It would have been better if I hadn't burned it."

"I think I might have helped with that." There was that blush again, she was just so damn cute when her face was bright pink.

"That is true. You did distract me."

"And I'm looking forward to the next distraction. But first, we have to talk about what's been going on."

"Really? Are you sure it can't wait?"

"No, it can't. I need to know everything that's been happening. It wouldn't surprise me if you know who it is but didn't realize it yet. I hope by asking the right questions, it might trigger something."

"I think I need more wine first. If that's okay?"

"You don't have to ask me."

"Are you sure? You've been awful bossy."

"No, Angel, not bossy. Protective. There's a difference."

"If you say so," she said and pushed her lower lip out in a pout. But she couldn't keep it up and giggled. Between the wine and exhaustion, her defenses were down. It should make it easier for her to respond to his questions without overthinking. But her nibbling on her lower lip was driving him crazy.

"I say so. But it can wait until we get dinner cleared."

The relief she felt at the short reprieve shone in her eyes and triggered a twinge of guilt. She'd had a rough few days or longer since he still didn't know everything. Letting her off the hook wouldn't help her in the long run. Her safety was all that mattered, even if it meant a few hours of being unhappy.

Between them, they made quick work of the dishes and tossed the remains of the quiche in the trash. Then he refilled their wine glasses and carried them into her living room. Rori followed carrying one of the pink and black boxes she used in the bakery. He practically started drooling as soon as he saw it in her hands.

The lid of the box was open as she held it out for him to pick something. "The little squares are petit fours, basically little cakes with raspberry jam between layers of yellow cake and covered in fondant, umm icing. There are also mini-cream puffs and eclairs, and chocolate brandy balls. I wasn't sure what you'd like so I brought some of each."

Grabbing a petit four, he popped it in his mouth. If he kept this up, he'd gain ten pounds by the end of the first week. But damn it would be worth it. "Oh my God. That's delicious, thank you."

"You can have another. You're a big boy, no dessert restrictions since you ate your dinner."

"Smart ass," he said with a laugh. She was adorable. "and thank you, but not right now. I know what you're trying to do. But the longer you stall the later it's going to be before you can get some rest."

"Are you sure it can't wait until tomorrow?"

"I want to get out in front of this before the next thing happens. To do that I need more information."

"Fine. But there's not much to tell. What do you want to know?"

He took out his phone and opened the note app. "When did you open the bakery?"

"A little over a year ago."

"And when did the trouble start? Was it right away?" Dammit, she was nibbling on her lip again. He stood up in the guise of reaching for his wineglass, but he needed to adjust his jeans, or he was going to pass out from lack of circulation. If this went on much longer his cock was going to have permanent zipper marks.

"Umm, I can't remember exactly. I thought most of the stuff was just a coincidence."

"Like what? Try to remember, anything will help."

"Hmm. I had the grand opening in April, just before Easter and it went off without a hitch. I was still getting the apartment renovated then, so I was still living at my parent's house."

"Okay, good. Now think, what was the first thing that wasn't right?"

"I think it was in June. I started having trouble receiving my deliveries."

"You couldn't place the orders?"

"No. I'd make them the same way I'd been doing it all along, but somehow they'd end up being canceled. It was frustrating. There'd be days I had to run to Publix to pick up what I needed."

"Did it happen a lot?"

"For a couple of weeks, then I changed suppliers and things straightened out."

"And it didn't start up again with the new supplier?"

"No, the orders were fine after that. But then there was the trouble with the delivery van and my car. First, it was flat tires and then a dead battery. I had the garage on speed dial until I moved in here."

"And once you moved in the trouble with the car and van stopped?"

"With the car yes, because I left it at the house in the garage for now. So, I guess it's okay. I haven't been out there in a while. But I've had to get the tires fixed on the van at least three times."

"And you thought that was a coincidence?"

"I've been so busy. I honestly didn't think about it. I haven't had to make a lot of deliveries, so I don't pay attention until I need to use it."

"Gotcha. Is that it or have there been other things?"

"After I moved in here, I started getting phone calls all hours of the day and night. I'd just fall asleep when the phone would ring."

"Your cell phone?"

"No, it was the bakery number. I had the

phone line run up here too so I wouldn't miss any orders. But I shut the ringer off after the second night of calls. It really seemed like something teenagers would do. You know? So, I didn't give it much thought."

"Are you still getting the calls?"

"Usually once or twice a day. Not sure if they're still calling at night since the ringer is off."

"Did you get a call today?"

"Actually, no, I didn't. That's weird."

"Maybe not. It's the first time you weren't alone in the bakery, right? What do they say when they call?"

"Yes, that's true. You're the first 'helper' I've had there. It started out as just hang ups Then the line would be quiet for a few seconds before they'd hang up. But over the last few months, it changed. They'd spew hate and call me names. But the voice is weird. It doesn't sound like a person. Kind of robotic. I have no idea if they are male or female."

"They probably used a voice-modifier. Can you remember what they said? The words they used?"

"The most used one was whore, telling me I

should have been the one to die. Things like that."

"And you didn't tell anyone?"

"No, why would I?"

"The better question is why wouldn't you?"

"Because it just seemed like kids pulling pranks."

"I'm not buying it. The whole 'you should have been the one to die' instead? That doesn't seem like teenagers. That sounds personal."

"Maybe. I don't like to think about it and just try to put it out of my head."

"The other thing that bothers me is why now? Something had to trigger it. You were back in Willow Haven for almost a year before you opened the bakery, weren't you? Then another six months until you opened?"

"Yes, that sounds right. It took a while to find the right location, buy the property and then get it renovated."

"And nothing happened in the beginning?"

"No, nothing. It was pretty quiet until the reporter from one of the Orlando TV stations came out to interview me. Somehow they found out I'd survived the Paris terrorist attacks. They wanted to know everything about me, and they highlighted the bakery. It got really crazy for a while after that."

"When was this?"

"The beginning of June, before the issues with the deliveries started."

"Did the caller ever mention the TV interview?"

"No, not that I can remember." He knew he was pushing her, but there was something more going on than just a bunch of teenagers acting up. It was definitely personal.

"Has anyone given you a hard time since you've been back? Or problems from when you lived here before you went to Paris?"

"No, everyone is sweet, and they have all been so supportive."

"Okay."

"After the interview, it was kind of crazy. The bakery's Facebook page went viral. I had orders coming in from all over the country. I had to explain I wasn't set up to handle that type of business. I'd have made a killing but there was no way I could have handled all of that."

"I'd bet good money that whoever this is found out from the TV interview or Facebook.

That had to be the trigger. Now we need to find out the who and the why. What bothers me is the reference about you dying. Are you sure they said instead?"

"Yeah, it's what they said. It tore me up inside. My parents only flew to Paris to celebrate my graduation from the *Cordon Bleu*. Jim proposed right before all hell broke loose. If it weren't for me, they'd still be alive." Tears filled her eyes and spilled over and ran down her cheeks. It was his undoing.

"No, Angel, you're wrong. Shit just happens, this world is fucked up. So much hatred, too much hatred. I saw it every day for the last ten years. You did nothing wrong. I bet your parents couldn't have been prouder of you. And Jim? He was there anyway, you said you met him in Paris, right? It was just chance. It's always just chance when things happen. But there is no way you're to blame. If anyone bears the blame it's the terrorists. No one should have died or been injured."

He hadn't even realized he'd moved from the chair to the couch until he pulled her onto his lap and wrapped her in his arms. Whether she realized it or not, she'd given him a lot to go on. Tomorrow he'd call Chase and have him get Alex to comb through her social media. Alex was practically a genius when it came to computers and if he needed backup they had Rock. There were definite advantages to working for Eagle Security and Protection and being close to home base.

"I think it's time to get you to bed. You're exhausted."

CHAPTER 10

"**I**'m sorry."

"Again, you have nothing to be sorry for, sweetheart. You were an innocent in the wrong place at the wrong time. As were your parents and Jim. Trust me, I've seen it happen in more places than you'd believe. The world is changing. So much hatred."

"I know, but..."

"Shh, no buts."

Wrapped in his arms, she finally stopped shivering. Not that she was cold, it was struggling to hold back the tears. She'd forgotten about the TV interview and phone calls. How could she have forgotten? Especially when *that* night was crystal clear with every detail permanently etched in her memory.

The pounding of his heart beneath her ear helped to ease her tears. As she concentrated on the steady rhythm, she took a few deep breaths, and the tears gradually subsided.

"Better now?" Jasper asked as he kept her cocooned in his embrace. It was like being wrapped in a big warm blanket. Her eyes were getting heavy, and she yawned.

"Yes, just tired."

"I'm sorry I made you dredge up all those memories. But it was the only way to try to figure this out."

"I know. I really do. But it's much easier to try to keep it all buried. Or at least a lot less painful."

"But locking it all away is the worst thing you could do. You need to give yourself permission to heal, to live again. I don't know about Jim, but I can guarantee your parents wouldn't want you feeling guilty."

"You're right. Neither would Jim. He was so full of life."

"That reminds me. What was Jim's full name?"

"James Marshall, the third I think. I might have that number wrong. It could be the fourth. He didn't use it often. He wanted as much distance from his family as possible."

"You mentioned the family business. Do you know what it was?"

"It's a law firm, been around for ages, but I don't know any details since he wouldn't talk about it. I thought it was weird at first, but then we were so happy it didn't matter. I never even met them."

He pulled out his phone and typed something, but she was too tired to even try to see what he'd written. Then he stood with her in his arms.

"Hey, put me down. What are you doing?"

"Taking you to bed."

"I can walk."

"Yes, I know you can, but humor me. I'm not going to take advantage of you. We already went over that."

The desire to stand up for herself and demand he put her down, was not as strong as the desire to stay in his arms. He'd picked her size fourteen body up without any effort at all. Made her feel light as a feather as he carried her to her room. Snuggling closer, she sighed with contentment. This was probably a mistake, but she didn't have the energy to care.

Once they got to her room, he gently put her down. "I'm going to make sure we're all locked up and clear up the rest of the dishes. I'll be back to check on you." Then he dropped a soft kiss on her forehead and left her alone. The kiss was nothing like the passionate ones earlier, and a pang of disappointment squeezed her heart.

"Okay." She changed into her PJs, brushed her teeth, and had just climbed into bed when he returned.

"I brought some water in case you get thirsty."

"Thank you, that is very sweet." His eyes met hers, and she wondered what he was thinking. What would he say if she asked him to stay with her? Would he make love to her? He said she could set the pace, but after seeing her red blotchy face in the bathroom mirror, she couldn't believe anyone would want her.

"I'm sorry I upset you. I hope you can get some sleep. I'll see you in the morning, Angel."

His lips met hers in a brief kiss but as he straightened she grabbed his hand.

"Could you stay? At least until I fall asleep."

"Of course." He sat on the edge of the bed and took off his sneakers. Then he stretched out on top of the covers and pulled her against his side. She turned toward him and rested her head on his chest, the thud of his heartbeat helped her relax.

"Thank you, Jasper," she mumbled. Her eyes were so heavy, and she couldn't fight off sleep any longer. "Night."

She thought she heard him answer but she wasn't sure.

"**G**ood night, my sweet angel."

She was everything he never knew he wanted. He'd dated more than his share over the years, but they'd never pulled on his heart-strings. Hell, he'd forgotten most of their names before they'd left his bed. He wasn't proud of it, but he'd never promised them anything. Never planned to settle down. Delta Force had been his life. There wasn't room for anything else. Or hadn't been until Paris when a little woman with huge blue eyes burrowed into his heart and refused to leave.

After all the dead ends he'd run into, he'd been about to give up on ever finding her again. It was strange how the universe worked. Chase believed that everything happened for a reason, maybe he was right. What were the odds he'd go to work for him and end up meeting the woman who had haunted his life for the last two years? He wouldn't have taken that bet. But there he was, with Rori's head lying on his chest, and her body curled around his.

Pulling the clip holding up her hair, he put it on the nightstand and ran his hands through her curls releasing the scent of her pineapple shampoo. Soft, and fluffy. It had been the truth when he'd told her he wanted her. It was torture having her soft body wrapped around him. He hadn't been with a woman in longer than he could remember, and now the one he wanted was within reach but strictly off limits.

When he was sure she was asleep, he gently slid out from under her. He'd have loved to stay, but it was only nine and he needed to give Chase a call to see if he could check out a few things. He was used to functioning on only a few hours of sleep, and as long as he was in bed by midnight, he'd be fine.

Stopping by his room, he grabbed his laptop and sat at the kitchen table. After transferring his notes from his phone to the computer, he gave Chase a call.

"Brennan."

"Hey, Chase."

"How did the rest of the day go? Any more trouble?"

"It was okay. But she wouldn't go out for dinner. Today really shook her."

"I'm not surprised. Willow Haven is not exactly immune to that kind of thing, but it's not really common either. Did Steele find out anything at all?"

"Not that he told me. I figured you'd hear before I do, he's your brother. But I'm hoping you can have Alex or Rock do some digging for me. They're much better at that shit."

"No problem. Whatever you need. What did you find out?"

"The trouble started after a TV reporter interviewed her. Do you remember when they came here? Rori said it went viral on social media. After that the harassment started and has continued for the last six months, she just didn't bother to tell anyone. She is one hell of a stubborn woman. If Lily hadn't been there when the window was shattered she'd probably have found a way to keep that quiet too."

"Any thoughts on who might be behind it?"

"No, that's what I need your help with. I think it's either someone fixated on her from the interview or who knew her or her fiancé."

"It was Jim something, right?"

"James Marshall, the third or the fourth, she wasn't one hundred percent sure. The family is on the east coast somewhere, old money and run a law firm. But Jim was a journalist in Paris. Rori never met his family. Hell, they came to Paris to retrieve his body and bring it back home and they never even stopped by the hospital to check on her. It just feels off to me."

"Understood. Send me anything else you come up with, and we'll start working it in the morning. If there's dirt out there, Alex will find it."

"I'm counting on it."

"Don't be surprised if you have more of us stopping by tomorrow."

"I won't, I figured you'd be all over this one since she's a home town girl."

"Exactly. Hell, I knew her when she was younger and her parents too. She's become our own little celebrity here. Like you said, the TV coverage and social media made her famous or infamous. Snowbirds and tourists come here and visit the bakery."

"She deserves good to happen to her, not all this fucked up shit."

"And that's why you're on the job. I know you'll keep her safe. Steele and Ethan are doing what they can. But so far as you saw for yourself, there's not a lot to go on. But hopefully, Alex will be able to dig some stuff up."

"I sure hope so. I don't want to wait until the guy fucks up to catch him."

"Exactly. I'll get back to you tomorrow."

CHAPTER 11

Rori woke just before her alarm went off. Disappointed that Jasper wasn't still in bed with her, she couldn't blame him. She'd only asked him to stay until she fell asleep. It was probably for the best considering her dreams had been filled with him. They'd made love in the bakery and were covered in chocolate frosting. It's no wonder she'd looked for him the moment she opened her eyes.

Glancing at the clock, she'd already wasted ten minutes daydreaming about her sexy stud muffin man. It was time to get busy or she would be behind all day. After showering and getting dressed in record time, she quietly snuck past Jasper's door to get to the kitchen and make the coffee. It felt like a Hawaiian Kona type of day and he'd said he didn't care as long as it was coffee. Hopefully, he'd enjoy her favorite bean.

"Good morning."

"Morning," she answered as she turned toward him with a smile. At least he hadn't snuck up on her.

"Did you sleep well?"

"Yes, but that was going to be my question."

"I slept fine. Thank you for staying with me."

"You are so adorable when you sleep, Angel. I hated to leave, but I needed to get some work done."

"Did you come up with anything?"

"Not yet. But I have Chase and Alex working on some things. With any luck, we'll turn up something we can use. We'll catch the asshole, don't worry."

She wasn't worried about him catching the person, it was what would happen afterward. It was how his job worked. Assignments wherever they had clients. Lily was lucky that Alex was the computer geek, so he stayed put in Willow Haven. But Jasper wasn't the stay put type.

Would she just be another job to him after it was over?

"I'm not worried. Ready to head downstairs?"

"Yup." She handed him his coffee and grabbed hers then headed for the door. It felt so normal for him to be there and it had only been one day. How would it feel after a week or longer if they couldn't catch whoever was stalking her?

As they stepped outside the floodlight came on and startled her. She'd forgotten he'd installed it, but now she knew it worked. There was no way anyone would sneak up on her in the dark. It was practically daylight it was so bright.

"That is really bright."

"It's supposed to be. I don't want anyone being able to surprise you. I put some cameras in too."

"Cameras, like surveillance?"

"Yup. I figured then if someone tosses another rock or brick or decides to have fun with spray paint we'll have them in living color."

"Where did you put them?" she asked as she unlocked the back door of the bakery.

"One back here, a couple in the front of the shop, outside the front, the hallway going up to your apartment in case they actually get through the door. Then at least you'll know who is outside of your door before you open it. I set up the monitors in my room, I need to set up the ones inside the bakery today."

"Don't you think that's overkill?"

"No, sweetheart, not where you're concerned. I don't want you to be afraid."

Not knowing what to say, she got to work. It was always a tight schedule to get everything done before she opened at six. The bread dough came first, followed by the different pastries and rolls. Then it was on to finishing the croissants, she'd started the day before. The routine was so ingrained in her she didn't have to think about it.

"What can I do to help?"

"Want to learn how to knead bread?"

"Need bread? I love bread, but I don't need it."

Laughing, she grabbed his hand and pulled him over to the breadboard. "This is what you do. You knead it with your knuckles like this. Then rotate it, knead again, fold it over, and knead it again. Then you put it into those pans and cover them with the clothes. Think you can handle that?"

"Yeah, no problem." He washed his hands and went to work. She watched for a bit and stopped him from mutilating the bread a couple of times before he got the hang of it. It was nice being able to move on to tackle the next thing on her list. Six a.m. arrived quickly and once again she had a line of customers waiting outside the door.

"Did I tell you they were coming to install the new window?

"No, when is that?"

"They didn't give me a set time just said today. I'll be happy to be able to see out again, I hate that piece of wood."

"I don't blame you. Do you want more coffee before we open up?"

"Thanks, that'd be great." She watched him walk into the bakery area and couldn't help admiring the buns of steel encased in his dark blue jeans. Which then led to remembering the view of his chest. It was rock hard, chiseled and badly scarred. But it didn't detract from his beauty at all. If she didn't watch it, she'd be drooling all over the counter.

Jasper handed her the coffee and took a drink of his. "Anything out of the ordinary happening today?"

"Besides the window? Just finishing up a wedding cake I've been working on. It needs to be delivered to Ruby's B&B tomorrow. The Evanston's are renewing their vows – fifty years. Can you believe it? Anyway, she ordered the wedding cake since they didn't have one when they first got married."

"You said you started it?"

"Yup, the cake is baked, and the first layer of fondant is on. It still needs the fancy stuff which will take me most of the day. Luckily, I have you to help.

"You want me to help decorate a wedding cake? Are you sure that's such a good idea?"

"You won't be decorating, you'll be handling the customers out front. All you have to do is yell if you need me."

"What would you have done if I wasn't here?"

"I don't know, probably beg Lily or Anna to come and help out? I suppose I'm going to have to consider hiring someone soon. It's getting too busy for me to do it all alone. So, what do you say, think you can handle the front of the bakery by yourself?"

"Only if you promise not to unlock the back door or leave the shop."

"I promise. I'll be too busy to do anything else."

"What time tomorrow does it have to be delivered?"

"Four, so we'll have time to close up and drive it over there. Ruby's is only a couple of blocks away. I'm hoping that I can get most of it done. But if not, tomorrow will be a repeat of today."

Before they could say anything else, the jingling bells on the front door let them know they had customers.

The day flew by. He didn't know how she managed the bakery by herself. There was a steady stream of customers and half of them wanted to chat. Yesterday they must have been checking him out because today was one question after another. Why was he there, was he Rori's boyfriend, how long was he staying? It went on and on. He kept to the cover story that he was a distant relative of Lily's and was helping Rori out. It placated most of the curious, and they went off to compare notes. Or at least, that's what he figured they were doing. But late afternoon a guy came in and sort of hung back in the corner of the bakery. Jasper tried to make eye contact, but he avoided him. While Jasper helped a couple of women buying a bunch of the petit four things for a book club meeting, the guy wandered around. He never said a word, just casually wandered around and scoped out the bakery. There was something off about the guy and his attitude. It didn't feel right.

As he packaged up the tiny delicious squares, he tried to keep an eye on him. After finally finishing with the chatty women, he prepared to confront the guy but when he looked around the man had left. Worried he'd managed to get past him and into the kitchen, he stole a look into the back to make sure Rori was okay.

Relieved to see her hard at work on the

confectionary masterpiece that she called a cake, he stood and stared. He'd never seen anything so beautiful made of sugar, except maybe his Angel. She had quite a bit of the white stuff on her as well.

It wasn't long after that the window installers arrived and mounted the new window faster than he'd expected and with little disruption of the bakery traffic. Getting rid of the plywood allowed him better visibility of the area and let in the sunlight making the patisserie a cheery place. It was hard to believe that four months ago he was knee deep in mud in Central America on a rescue mission. The mission that cost him his military career. Just thinking about it made the muscles in his thigh ache, a less than gentle reminder that he'd been standing on it all day.

The last hour was slow, customers dwindled in and by two-thirty it was dead. Three o'clock couldn't get there fast enough for him. Emails had come in from Chase and Alex but up until then, he hadn't had time to read them. After locking the door, he went to check on his little pastry chef extraordinaire.

"How's it going?"

"Great. What do you think?" She backed away from her masterpiece to give him his first full view of the cake.

"Holy shit. You made all those flowers?"

"Yup. Everything is edible. I think it came out well."

"It's fantastic. Mrs. Evanston is going to be head over heels for the cake."

"Now we just have to deliver it tomorrow without any catastrophes. I figured since we didn't have far to go I could risk putting it together for the delivery."

"It's not usually like this?"

"Nope, it's delicate this way, or extra delicate I guess. Usually, I leave it in a couple of pieces and do the final assembly at the wedding site."

"Have you made a lot of these?"

"This is only my third, but I love it. Like making something magical to complement their special day. Maybe someday I'll make my own."

"I'm sure you will." No sooner had the words left his lips when he wanted to kick his own ass. He really needed to think before he opened his big mouth. But the eyes she lifted to meet his weren't sad as he'd expected. Instead, hope was reflected back at him, and it eased the painful twisting of his heart. The last thing he wanted to do was bring her pain. If she could open her heart again, maybe he could convince her to give it to him. He'd make sure the rest of her life was as magical as the cake.

"Maybe. Okay, let's get this beauty into the walk-in. I still have to make the croissant dough for tomorrow and more custard for the eclairs. Then get this place cleaned up before I can really say I'm done."

CHAPTER 12

A bit nervous about leaving Jasper alone in the front of the bakery, she'd checked on him a few times in the morning. But seeing that he had it under control, she let her creative juices take over. It wasn't until her shoulders started yelling at her, that she realized she'd been at it non-stop for hours.

Wedding cakes were the one time she could really use her imagination especially if the customer didn't have any specific requirements, which Mrs. Evanston hadn't. She'd been thrilled that Rori had agreed to make it on such short notice. If she hadn't had Jasper there helping her she would have been up all night working on the elaborate cake and its tiers of flowing lilies and roses, delicate spun sugar hearts and green ivy vines. It might be her best creation yet and she'd have to remember to take some pictures to add to her book.

By the time Jasper had locked up the front of the bakery, she was putting the finishing touches on the cake. Stepping back to check for gaps in the flowers or ivy, she carefully spun the cake when she heard a low whistle behind her and smiled.

"What do you think?"

"I think Mrs. Evanston is going to be head over heels for it."

After they got it into the walk-in, she had to complete her usual close out list starting with the croissant dough. It was one of the most time-consuming items she made on a daily basis, but it was also her best seller.

"Can I help with anything?"

"Would you be up for stirring custard?"

"Yeah, I think I can handle that."

"It's important you keep a steady stir, or it won't turn out right."

"You get it started and I'll keep it going."

Grateful she could cross off an extra item from her list, she pulled out the ingredients to make her custard. She made a huge batch each time since it was used for the eclairs, crème puffs, and the filling for some of her cakes. Once it was set up, she handed the spoon to Jasper and got to work on the croissant dough.

The phone rang as soon as she was up to her elbows in flour. "Typical. It has to happen at least once a week. I swear it's like there is a pressure point on the floor. When I step on it the phone rings, and it's always at the worst possible moment," Rori said as she grabbed a towel and wiped the dough and flour off her hands before walking over to grab the phone.

"Want me to get it?"

"Nope, you need to keep stirring or it will get lumpy. I've got it."

By the time she got to the phone, whoever it was had hung up. Again, typical. But she kept forgetting to leave the phone near where she was working.

"No one there?"

"I think I was just too late. If they want something they'll call back."

"You're not worried about losing a customer?"

"No. Everyone in town knows I work by myself. I don't think it would put them off. Besides, they could leave a voicemail."

Jasper nodded as he continued to stir but looked like he wanted to say more.

"Something wrong?"

"No, just thinking about…" Before he could finish whatever he was going to say the phone rang again.

"See, I told you," she said with a grin before she pushed on the answer button. "Prince's Patisserie, may I help you?"

"You don't really think having that guy there will save you, do you? Because you'd be dead wrong, accent on the dead."

"Who are you? Why are you doing this?" Jasper grabbed the phone from her hand.

"Listen, fucktard. You need to back off. Leave Aurora and her bakery the fuck alone or you will be sorry."

"Really? Whatcha gonna do? You think you're all high and mighty ex-Delta. You're not so much hot shit. You better watch your ass because if you stand in our way we'll take you out too."

"What did they say?" Rori asked as Jasper put the phone on the counter. "Did you hang up on them?"

"Nope, he hung up, if it was a 'he.' I'm not entirely sure. They were using a modulator to disguise their voice like I figured."

"And that's the reason it sounds like that?"

"Yes, most likely. Is that usually how the calls are?"

"Mostly. In the beginning, it was just breathing. The caller ID always shows up as anonymous. I wouldn't answer those, but I have customers whose numbers also show up that way."

"Right. Maybe you should let me get the phone while I'm here. If it's a legitimate call I'll hand you the phone."

It was the smart thing to do, but her pride wanted to yell, 'no, I can answer my own damn phone.' But he was there to protect her. Why was she fighting him so hard on each little thing he wanted to do to keep her safe? It freaked her out every time they called, and it was definitely worse this time. "Okay."

"Really? From the look on your face, I thought you were going to object."

"I almost did," she replied with a smile. "But you'd just bully me into submission anyway."

"Is that what you think I'm doing? Bullying you?"

"No, not really. I'm sorry."

"Don't apologize, Angel. I need to know if that's what you think. Because it's the last thing I'd ever do. I am just trying to keep you safe. I watched the color drain out of your face as you listened to whatever crap he was spouting. I don't know what that mother fucker said to you, but it was clear that you were scared."

"It was more threatening this time."

"Do you remember what he said?" Oh yeah, she remembered, it would take a while for that memory to fade.

"He said that you wouldn't be able to protect me. That I was dead wrong if I thought you could." She shivered after she said it. It sounded so ominous and she'd been there before. Caring about people and having them stolen from her way too soon. It was the real reason she didn't want to let go of any control.

The last time she had, everything had been taken from her. There was no way she was going through that again.

There was something between them, lust for sure, but more, it was too early to really tell. But she couldn't bear to lose anyone else she cared about.

"You know that's not true, right? I can and will keep you safe. I promise."

"I'm not sure you should make that promise. We've both lived through things that shouldn't have happened, that left us scarred inside and out."

"But this is different. My sole job is to make sure you're safe. And even if I hadn't met you before I would be just as dedicated to my task. It has nothing to do with how I feel about you, and everything to do with your safety."

Rori nodded as she turned back to the dough. She wanted to believe him, but she couldn't. The threats were so personal and maybe they'd just wait him out. It's not like she could afford to cover his salary indefinitely and she would never consider not paying Chase's firm for their work. He wasn't running a charity.

"What are you thinking about now? I can practically see the wheels turning."

"You should be stirring that custard and not staring at my head. If there are lumps in there we'll have to toss it and start over."

"No lumps. But how do I know when it's done?"

Grabbing the towel, she wiped her hands as she walked over to the stove. Her world was off balance and nothing seemed right. She'd forgotten all about the custard and it was probably burned. Taking a peek into the pot it looked okay, but the true test was the flavor. Grabbing a spoon from the drawer, she dipped it into the pot and took a taste.

"Well, how is it? Did I destroy it?"

"Nope. It's perfect. You did a great job. Turn off the gas and move it to the back burner to let it cool a bit before we put it in the walk-in."

"Done. What can I do next?"

"Nothing. I just have to finish this up and do all the dishes."

"Let me do them." Again, he was just offering to help why was it so hard for her to say yes. Damn stubborn streak.

"Sure, go ahead. Thank you."

"See, was that so hard?"

As she turned back to the dough, she mumbled, "You have no idea."

It took another hour before they were all finished, and the bakery was locked up tight. It was crazy that she did this all by herself. It had to be sheer force of will. Rori was the definition of dynamo. The woman didn't know how to take a break. But it was catching up to her now. Or maybe it was all the stress of the stalker.

Thankfully there weren't any surprises greeting them outside. He'd been concerned when he remembered the weird guy who'd been casing the bakery earlier. It could have been to make sure they were both inside. He wished he'd had a chance to grab a picture of the guy before he'd ducked out.

"Why don't you shower first, or I might be tempted to lick all that sugar off of you."

"Yeah, I had a little fun with the confectioners' sugar when I was making the royal icing for the decorations."

Leaning down, he kissed her gently on the lips. "Yup, definitely good enough to eat." Her giggle was the response he'd hoped for. She was strung way too tight after the phone call on top of the long day.

"Are you sure you don't want to go first? I can start something for dinner."

"Don't worry about dinner. How about pizza? Then you can just relax tonight."

"Are you sure you don't mind? I know you don't get a lot of real food."

"Pizza is real food."

"Umm, not according to the *Cordon Bleu*. But sure, go for it. I can't remember the last time I had a slice."

"What do you like?"

"I'm easy, anything but pineapple and anchovies."

"No Hawaiian pizza then. Check. Okay. Go hop in the shower and I'll make sure you're not disturbed."

"Do you want money?"

"No, it's my treat. Besides, I know you brought something for dessert so I'm sure we'll be even. Now go. Before I drag you in there and help you."

Pink flooded her cheeks as she took off down the hallway. He heard the bathroom door shut and then called Chase.

"Brennan."

"Hey, Boss."

"How's it going, Raptor?"

"Well, Rori got a phone call this afternoon from the stalker. I couldn't tell if they're male or female, but they know way more information than they should."

"What do you mean?"

"They knew I was ex-Delta and that's classified intel. How the fuck did they find that out? It is also obvious they're watching her every move. They told her I couldn't keep her safe."

"How is she holding up?"

"She's tough, a fighter, but it's wearing on her. Honesty, I don't know how she's been handling everything on her own. It's a shit ton of work. Then with all stress of being stalked, I don't know how she's keeping it together."

"It's good you're there."

"Apparently. I haven't had a chance to read through all the info you and Alex sent yet, I'll check it out after dinner. Did he turn up anything on the boyfriend's family?"

"He's still digging, but he said there's something off about them. It looks like they might be connected to organized crime. Their financials are whacked."

"Okay, I'll go through what Alex sent and see if anything jumps out at me. There was a guy who came into the bakery this afternoon. He didn't buy a thing and when I was busy with other customers he slipped out. But he was definitely casing the place."

"Did you get a photo?"

"No, I fucked up. I was busy with customers and then he was gone. I'll check the footage from the cameras, maybe they caught something."

"If you turn up anything, forward the footage to Alex and Rock."

"Will do. Hey, before I let you go. Who delivers pizza around here?"

Chase laughed and then gave him the number to Genna's the local NY-style pizzeria. "Try their special coal-fired pizza. It's the best around."

"Thanks. I'll email you later if the video

shows anything or I have questions about the info you sent."

"You'd better. Let me know if you need anything or if Rori does. Faith said she'd be happy to come over and help out at the bakery."

"I'll let Rori know. Talk to you tomorrow."

"Night."

Taking Chase's recommendation, he ordered a medium coal-fired Genna's special and a large salad. He could have cared less about the green stuff, but he figured that Rori might appreciate some 'real' food with the pizza.

While waiting for dinner to be delivered, he set the table and opened a bottle of wine. He was just about to check on Rori when he heard the blow dryer. She'd been in the shower a lot longer than the night before and he was starting to worry.

The door buzzer rang, and he checked the video monitor before he headed downstairs to get the pizza. The delivery driver looked like he was still in high school, and Jasper took their order and gave him a big tip. Before he went back upstairs he checked the area, making sure nothing looked out of place.

Rori was waiting for him when he walked in with the pizza. "That smells heavenly."

"I told you pizza was real food. C'mon let's eat, I'll shower afterward. I'm starving."

"When aren't you?" she asked with a giggle.

CHAPTER 13

R ori hated to admit it but the pizza was delicious and nothing like she'd remembered. It had to be almost ten years at least. Jasper ordered the salad for her, but she'd barely touched it. Instead, she gobbled two of the overloaded slices.

"I take back everything I said about it not being real food. That was amazing."

"Yes, it was. You can thank Chase. He recommended this place. The coal-fired makes all the difference."

"I'll take your word for it. Thank you for buying me dinner."

"I'm glad you liked it and now we have leftovers for tomorrow. Bonus."

"Unless you eat it later. I've noticed that someone likes to raid the refrigerator after I've gone to bed."

"Who me?" His feigned innocence cracked her up. He was a piece of work. It was surprising how quickly she got used to having him around. She'd really expected it to be much more awkward than it had been.

"Yeah. Don't try to deny it. I don't sleepwalk and eat so that leaves you. Unless we've got some really big mice that can open the refrigerator."

"Maybe."

"Go take a shower. I'll clean this up. Maybe we can watch a movie before bed."

"Sounds good. I'll be back in a few."

As she cleared the table and brought everything into the kitchen, she could hear Jasper singing in the shower but couldn't make out the words. Slipping down the hall she listened outside the door and cracked up as he bellowed the song out loud and proud. Covering her mouth with her hand to stifle her laughter, she hurried back to the kitchen. Who'd have expected Mr. Stud Muffin to be singing *Girls Just Want to Have Fun*? Seriously?

"What's so funny?" He asked from behind her. He must have been at the end of his shower since it wasn't five minutes since she'd been giggling outside the door.

"Nothing," she answered with the trace of laughter still in her voice.

"Something wrong with my singing?"

"No, not at all. I was just a little surprised at your song choice."

As she answered, she turned to look at him and he took her breath away. He was barefoot, in faded blue jeans and an old Navy t-shirt that looked more like a second skin. It accentuated every curve of his six-pack. Her gaze traveled up his body taking in every glorious inch until she finally met his hazel eyes which were dancing with laughter. Blushing, she finished her inspection with his hair. It was just long enough to stick straight out from his head like some kind of a mad scientist. And her insides melted a little more. Head to toe he was the sexiest man she'd ever seen, and she prayed she wasn't drooling.

"What's wrong with *Girls Just Want to Have Fun?* You have something against Cyndi Lauper?"

"Nope, it's a great song just not one I expected to hear coming from my bathroom in baritone."

"What? Don't men usually sing in your shower? Anyway, I was just trying to get a reaction, preferably laughter."

"You were messing with me?"

"Maybe, just a little. It worked. Right?"

"Yeah, it did. But I'm not sure that's the truth. I think you're trying to protect your macho image and hoping I don't share your love of Cyndi Lauper with Lily. I'm surprised you didn't hear me laughing."

"I can hear a mouse fart a hundred yards away. So yeah, I heard you loud and clear," Jasper said as he puffed out his chest. How the shirt wasn't busting at the seams she had no idea.

"You know, payback is a bitch. One of these days when you least expect it…"

"Don't worry, Angel, I will always expect it."

"We'll see."

"Yes, we will. Now, how about that movie? And what did you pick for dessert? More of those little square thingies?"

"Nope, no petit fours tonight. I grabbed

something different. What do you think of these?" She handed him a coffee macaron and watched as he popped the whole thing in his mouth.

As he chewed the corners of his mouth turned up in a smile. "I like it. What do you call it?"

"A macaron."

"A macaroon? Aren't they usually coconut? I'm pretty sure I had those before, and they didn't taste like that."

"Macaroons are totally different. No coconut in these but there are a bunch of different flavors. Let me know which one you like best."

"So far I like them all," he mumbled with his mouth full. He had the box in his hand and was walking to the living room. She finished putting the last of the dishes in the dishwasher and followed him.

"Did you leave me any?"

He looked embarrassed as he held out the box. "Two? You only left me two? There were fifteen in that box."

"I told you I liked them."

Rori struggled not to laugh. He'd sworn he

didn't like sweets and yet he'd demolished every pastry she'd given him, it was hysterical. "It's okay. I brought them for you, but I didn't think you'd devour them in two minutes."

"What can I say? They were delicious and I couldn't resist."

"I'll remember that." She took out an imaginary pad and pretended to make a note while she said, "'don't bring Jasper delicious food if you don't want him to eat it all.' Got it."

"Hmm, maybe you better make a note about you too."

"What do you mean?"

Instead of answering her, he pulled her onto his lap and took possession of her lips. Surprise parted them and gave him the chance to slide his tongue into her mouth. With a purr, she sank further into his embrace. The feel of his lips and the taste of the macarons on his tongue set her body aflame and any thought of resistance evaporated. Desire coursed through her veins, as his hands slid through her hair then down her neck leaving a trail of heat wherever he touched her skin.

Then it was over, and he rested his forehead against hers. "I'm sorry. I can't seem to stop myself when it comes to you. But I promised to give you time."

Confused, disappointed, and with her heart racing, Rori struggled to come up with words. The loss of his touch left her bereft and unbalanced. Not sure how to react, she told herself she was tired and tense from everything that had been going on. But she was fooling herself. His kisses knocked her on her ass every time.

After taking a deep breath, she slid off of his lap. There was no way she could make sense of anything while they were so close. "I don't know what this is between us, but you have nothing to be sorry about. I could have stopped you. You didn't force me, not now, and not earlier."

"Maybe not, but it wasn't professional. I'm supposed to be keeping you safe not jumping your bones. Chase will have my ass in a sling. Fuck. Alex will probably sic Hunter on me." Oh yeah, that was a definite possibility and she grinned.

"It's none of their business. We're adults and we don't need anyone's permission."

"No, we don't, but romancing a client wouldn't put me at the top of the employee of the month list. But I can't seem to resist you. I want you. All of you. Every taste leaves me hungry for more."

Jasper's words stirred emotions she'd forgotten existed and her body quickened with excitement. He'd put her thoughts into words when she couldn't, but then she glimpsed Jim's picture on the bookcase. A rush of guilt cooled her passion and squeezed her heart. She'd loved him and believed with all of her heart that he had loved her. But he'd never taken her breath away, made her quiver at the slightest touch, or rattled her thoughts like Jasper. He was wreaking havoc on her feelings.

Everything was so messed up right now she didn't know which way was up. Fear was a powerful emotion. She'd learned that in Paris firsthand. Until the moment the gunfire erupted, she'd never known true fear and it had changed everything.

Even if she didn't admit it to anyone, she *was* scared. Maybe that's what was triggering the feelings—the attraction. There was a term for it, but she'd be damned if she could remember what it was. Now that he was in her life and protecting her, she felt safer than she'd been since Paris, so it was inevitable she'd feel something, right? Yes, she was working hard to come up with any reason for her reaction except the one she was desperately trying to ignore.

She had her bakery. It was enough, wasn't it? After she lost Jim, the plan had been to throw herself into work. No more relationships. But she couldn't seem to convince her hormones. The intense desire, craving his touch—it was unlike anything she'd felt before, and no matter how hard she tried, there was no denying it.

He could hear Chase's voice now. What the fuck was he doing? The last thing Rori needed were more complications. Keeping her safe and finding out who was behind all the shit happening in her life was his mission. That's where his focus needed to be instead of acting like some horndog drooling all over her. When he'd blurted out how he wanted her, he wasn't sure how she'd react. But the last thing he'd expected was no reaction at all. Instead, she was staring at him wide-eyed and nibbling her thumbnail. He could almost see she was trying to figure things out. It was up to him to get things back on track.

"What movie do you want to watch?"

"Huh?"

"Movie? We were going to watch one so you could relax before bed."

"Oh yeah. Umm, why don't you pick one? I'll go get us some wine. I know I could use it."

"Sounds good." It had been heaven having her in his arms, tasting her. He hadn't lied when he'd said he wanted all of her, but his timing sucked. He should be kicking his own ass. Instead, he perused her collection of movies. He approved of most of her choices, and his first instinct was to pick one of the Die Hard movies but figuring a chick flick would be a better choice, he grabbed the movie *Letters to Juliet* and popped it into the Blu-ray player. The opening credits were playing when Rori walked in with popcorn and two glasses of wine.

"Wow. A chick flick? I expected you to put in Die Hard or one of the Marvel movies."

"I thought you might appreciate this more. I've never seen it, and I figured if it was in your collection you liked it."

"I bet you'll be asleep in ten minutes."

"You're on. What do you want to bet?"

"Hmm, if you fall asleep you have to clean up the kitchen tomorrow."

"And if I don't, what do I get?"

"What do you want?" Damn, talk about a loaded question and he was trying to behave.

"How about you let me take you to the beach for a picnic?"

"Really? That's what you want?"

"It'll do for the time being. Now, how about you let me have some of the popcorn?"

She passed him the bowl and settled onto the couch. He'd half expected her to sit as far away from him as she could get and was pleasantly surprised when she snuggled against his side. It eased his worry that he'd upset her, and a self-satisfied grin spread across his face.

"What are you smiling about?"

"Nothing really. Just enjoying your company, and the popcorn. Although I could really go for a few more of those macarons."

"Oh my God, you're unbelievable."

"You're just now realizing that?" Before he had a chance to move, she'd elbowed him in the side. It hadn't hurt but it sure as hell made him laugh.

The movie wasn't half bad and ten minutes later he was still awake and won their bet, but he'd have to wait to tell her in the morning since Rori was fast asleep against his side. She looked so peaceful he hated to disturb her, but she'd be hating life in the morning if she slept like that all night.

Gently taking the popcorn bowl out of her lap and putting it on the coffee table, he scooped her into his arms and tried not to wake her. He made it down the hall and into her room before she stirred in his arms.

"What's going on?" she murmured still sounding half asleep.

"It's okay, Angel. I'm putting you to bed."

"Thank you." He smiled as he placed her on the bed and pulled her quilt over her. "Will you stay with me?"

"I'm not sure that's a good idea."

"Please? Just until I fall asleep." This seemed to be turning into a habit but there was no way he could say no. Just looking at her beautiful face, and her curly chestnut hair framing her wide blue eyes.

"Okay. Until you fall back to sleep." Her smile looked like the cat who ate the canary, and she moved over to make room for him. Hadn't he decided not an hour ago to keep their relationship professional until the job was over? His Delta brothers would never let him hear the end of this if they found out.

Jasper stretched out on the bed, and she cuddled against his side with a sigh of contentment. He slid his arm under her shoulders and pulled her closer. Her hand rested over his heart. The feisty little baker had his heart in her hand, literally and figuratively. Mission or not, he'd do anything for her, even if she asked him to walk away forever.

It didn't take long for Rori to fall back to sleep and as much as he enjoyed the feel of her body cuddled against him, Jasper had work to do, including reviewing the video to find the mystery man who'd been in the bakery.

After a gentle kiss on her forehead, he slid out of her embrace. Being careful not to make any noise, he waited a moment to make sure she was still sleeping, then left the door ajar. Jasper had to find out who was threatening his Angel and take care of them. For his own peace of mind, he needed to know she'd be safe even if he had to walk away from her.

While the video downloaded to his laptop, Jasper cleaned up the popcorn and washed the wine glasses. He didn't want Rori to have to do it at zero dark thirty when she got up for work. The woman was unbelievable. How she'd managed the bakery all on her own for so long, he had no idea. It was no wonder Chase was concerned. The woman was on a runaway train about to careen off the tracks if they didn't find the stalker and take some of the pressure off her shoulders soon.

The video didn't give him much. The guy wasn't some street thug from the way he knew to avoid the cameras and kept the hoodie pulled over his head. There were a few glimpses of the side of his face, but it wouldn't give Alex or Rock much to go on. Making notes to send with the link to the video, he was on the third replay when he heard a soft whimper. Pausing the video, he went to check on Rori. He was halfway between the kitchen and her room when she screamed. His gun was out of its holster and the safety off before he raced into her room.

CHAPTER 14

A quick check of Rori's room told him it was empty except for his Angel. Stowing the gun, he sat down on the edge of her bed. Stroking the side of her damp face until her eyes fluttered open, he was hoping to bring her out of whatever horror she was experiencing.

"Angel? Rori, are you okay?"

"No. Please no. Oh God. Please don't. Oh God." The words were barely above a whisper. She was still in the grasp of the nightmare and he had to get her out of it.

"Angel?" When she still didn't answer and just looked at him with wide terrified eyes, he pulled her across his lap and cuddled her in his arms. "You're okay, it's just a dream. You're safe. I promise no one will hurt you."

Rori leaned into his chest, her body shaking as she sobbed. Not sure if she shook from fear or the force of her tears, he rested his chin against her head and whispered over and over that she was safe while he rocked her.

Her tears ripped his heart to shreds. It was one hell of a nightmare to leave her this shattered. A sickening thought slid through him, that it was his fault. Seeing him again couldn't have been easy and probably stirred up memories she'd put away. He'd been so relieved to have found her that he hadn't considered what it might do to Rori.

The tears and shaking slowed. "I'm sorry."

"For what, Angel? You didn't do anything wrong."

"It's happened before. The nightmare, I mean. It was…"

"My fault."

"What? What do you mean your fault?"

"I'm sure seeing me again stirred up all kinds of ugly you tried to forget."

"No, it wasn't your fault. I have them all the time. A lot more than I like. It used to be every night, now not so much. I'm sure all this stuff hasn't been helping."

"And you didn't think you should tell anyone?"

"Why? They're just dreams. They've gotten better. At first, I had them every night."

Jasper swore under his breath. Didn't she realize she had PTSD? It affected more than just the military. She'd experienced a traumatic event.

"Because if you talked to someone they could help you deal with the dreams and more."

"What more?

"Angel, you have PTSD. You might not realize it, but you have the signs."

"You're wrong." It wasn't the time to discuss this. She should be sleeping, getting rest for whatever was going to be thrown in their path tomorrow.

"Okay, I'm sorry. Do you think you can get back to sleep?"

"I don't know. Most of the time I just get up and go down to the bakery."

"You've only been sleeping for about two hours. How about a massage? I've been told I'm quite good at it." He felt her smile against his chest. At least he'd finally said something right.

"You've been told, hmm?"

"Yup. I've been told I'm better than the spa." The punch line had the effect he'd been going for as she giggled.

"I guess it couldn't hurt to try."

"Good choice. If you tell me where your lotion is, the one that smells great, I'll use that. Then you can lie down and lift your nightshirt."

"You're really observant, aren't you?"

"Angel, my life has depended on it more than once."

"It's the bottle of vanilla sugar body lotion in the nightstand drawer," she answered as she slid out of his lap and moved into the middle of the bed on her stomach. He struggled to hold back a groan as she lifted her shirt exposing more of her than he'd seen, and her soft skin appeared to glow in the moonlight.

The aroma permeated the room as he squeezed the lotion into the palm of his hand. No wonder she always smelled like sugar cookies. After letting the lotion warm up a bit in the palm of his hand, he gently spread it across her back. As he worked it into her shoulders, the tension slowly eased.

"You are good at this."

"I told you."

"Do I want to know where a Delta team member picked up this skill?"

"It's classified."

"That's not fair. You could say that all the time and I'd never know if it's the truth."

Jasper chuckled. "True, but in this case, it really is classified." He worked on the muscles in her neck and shoulders, then slowly moved down her back. Spending extra time at her shoulder blades and then down her spine to just above her hips.

"I'm definitely feeling more relaxed."

"That was the plan."

"My shoulders are still a bit tight."

"Okay, let me work on them some more." As he reached for the bottle she turned over onto her back. That wasn't part of the plan and he groaned. "I thought you wanted me to work on your shoulders?"

"I do, but from the front." She'd lifted her nightshirt off and was lying there in just her panties.

"You're killing me, Angel."

"I want you to finish what you started while we were on the couch."

"Are you sure? I don't want you to have any regrets."

"Dammit, Jasper, are you going to make me beg?" That was all he needed to hear, it had taken every ounce of self-control not to touch her gorgeous breasts or nibble on her nipples. His Angel was sheer perfection with perfectly rounded curves in all the right places. He liked his women with padding. It gave him more to love.

He told himself he'd take it slow to give her a chance to change her mind, but like most plans, it went sideways as soon as he touched her.

I f he'd held off one more minute she would have lost it. It was wonderful that he was worried about her, but what else could she say. Maybe it was too soon, but after all the things happening in her life did she really want to wait? It's not like she was a child or a virgin, and her body certainly had no doubt about what it wanted.

Rori could barely see his expression in the moonlight, but she did see him close his eyes. It was that moment when she knew he couldn't resist. Less than a heartbeat later he'd straddled her hips and his large calloused hands slid over her breasts. His rough fingertips rubbed back and forth over her nipples and she squirmed underneath him, arching up against his hands, silently begging for more.

"Tell me what you want, Angel."

"Everything…" Jasper's smile was wide and devilish in the dim light, as he lowered his head and his lips met hers, taking ownership, branding her as his forever. Every touch sent her closer to the edge. It was as if he'd flipped a switch making every inch of her more sensitive and stoked the flames of her passion higher and higher.

The kiss left her craving more and she whimpered when he released her. But it was only to move down her body. Thankful it was dark, so he wouldn't see her scars, she shut down her mind, and just let the feelings take over.

With lips, fingers, and tongue he worshiped her body from her mouth to her tummy and then he stopped. Aching for his touch she searched for him in the darkness, but he'd only gotten up to pull off his jeans. Then he was back, this time spreading her thighs. He slid down the bed and then buried his face against her, as his beard rubbed against her most private parts she had to bite down on her lip to keep from crying out.

Then his tongue swiped against her clit. It was all it took for her to come. Her juices poured from her onto the bed as her muscles contracted, aching for something to hold on to. "Jasper, oh God."

But he didn't stop, he continued to lick, suck and nibble until she orgasmed twice more. Ultra-sensitive nerves sent shivers of heat through her body with every touch.

"Please, I need you inside me."

"With pleasure, Angel. This may hurt a bit, if it does, tell me and we'll stop. You feel really tight and I'm on the large side."

"I don't care, make me yours." His groan against her clit sent shivers up her spine. Sitting up, he pulled her legs over his thighs and put his hands under her butt and lifted her. He could have hung her upside down from the ceiling at that point, whatever, as long as he was inside of her.

"If it hurts tell me." She didn't answer, there was no room for thought, only pleasure, and as he rubbed his hard dick against her she almost came again. Every muscle in her body twitched with desire, and as he eased into her vagina, she arched up against him pushing him further inside. It hurt and she felt so full, but it was intense and amazing, and she never wanted it to stop.

As he thrust inside her, again and again, he took one of her nipples into his mouth and sucked it hard, running his tongue over the tip. It was all it took to send her over the edge again except this time he followed right behind her, moaning her name as he came.

He pulled her with him as he stretched out on the bed, with her on top of him. This time she straddled his thighs and he reached up and grabbed both breasts as she rode him. Being on top was a new sensation and sent her over the edge again.

"I can't…"

"Come down here, Angel," Jasper murmured as he pulled her onto his chest and wrapped her in his arms. She must have drifted off because when she opened her eyes he'd lit some candles and he was watching her with a look of admiration while she was tucked against his side.

"What's that look for?"

"You really have no idea how amazing you are, do you?"

"I'm not…"

"Shhh. You are, and if it takes all night, I'm going to prove it."

They couldn't have been asleep more than ten minutes before the alarm sounded. She hurt in all the right places and was exhausted, but she wouldn't have changed one minute of it.

CHAPTER 15

It had been non-stop since they'd opened. The line seemed extra-long, or maybe it was just that she was dragging from lack of sleep. But oh man, was it worth it. Rori didn't think anything could knock the smile off her face. She was sure everyone who saw her could tell she had sex, but she didn't care. Jasper had moves she didn't know existed. Sneaking a glance at him as he waited on customers, she couldn't believe how they'd spent the night. They'd made love in more ways than she'd known were possible, and the soreness between her legs reminded her just how much he'd taught her. She'd thought his six-pack was something, but holy crow when his jeans came off she wasn't sure he'd fit. He was built like one of the heroes in her novels, except he was real.

The two of them were running on caffeine and the high from an amazing night of sex, but now that the day was over she was feeling it. Thank God she'd finished the wedding cake yesterday.

"Okay, that was the last customer. I locked up the front. What's next? The usual?"

"First up is delivering the cake, it needs to be there by four. I don't want to hold up the reception, these people aren't getting any younger."

Jasper snorted. Oh my God, it was so snarky. One night of mind-blowing sex and she was a new woman. She liked this version of herself. Hopefully, she hadn't shocked him too much.

"I can't believe you just said that."

"I can be horrible at times. But I try to behave around other people."

"I like this feisty version of you. I'll have to keep you up all night screaming my name more often."

"I guess we'll have to see. Can you back the van up to the rear door? It'll be easier if we don't have to carry it too far."

"Will do. But I'll carry the cake. You stay

inside until I come back in, okay? I want to be able to keep an eye on you."

"I think you're over-reacting. Nothing happened all day."

"Yeah well, we haven't been outside since four a.m. either."

While he went to move the van, she rinsed out the coffee urns and packed up some more macarons for their picnic. He'd won the bet and dinner would be a picnic on the beach.

"The van is as close to the door as I can get it. Ready?"

"Yeah. But be careful with that. I can't whip up a new one."

"Don't worry." Jasper picked up the huge cake and she followed him outside and watched as he carefully put it into the built-in box she'd had custom made. After he closed the doors they got into the van. He'd wanted to drive, but she insisted it was easier for her since she knew where they were going. Thankfully he'd given in.

Taking the turn from the parking lot onto Main Street was a slow process, but Rori wasn't going to take any chances with the cake. Then not even two seconds later, as soon as the van was out of the parking lot, Jasper yelled, "stop." She hit the brake pedal, but nothing happened. They didn't slow down, didn't stop, the van just kept going.

"There's something wrong. It won't stop." Thank God it was too early for rush hour, even in Willow Haven when it hit five p.m. there were a lot of cars on Main Street. Then she remembered the traffic light about a mile up the road. Panic churned in her stomach. Breaking out in a cold sweat, she was about to freak out. What if she hit someone? "What do I do about the light?"

"It's okay, Angel. Just hold on and listen to my voice. We're going to turn, and when I say turn, don't think just do it. Okay?" His hand covered hers on the steering wheel, and his calm helped ease some of her panic. Poor Mrs. Evanston was never going to have her wedding cake. "Rori, concentrate. I swear you're going to be okay. Just focus on my voice and do what I ask."

"Okay. I'm trying."

"I know, and you're doing a great job. Just hold on for a little longer. I'm going to pull the emergency brake. The van should slow down, but it might pull to one side. Are you ready?"

"I think so."

"Okay, hold on. I'm engaging the brake now." Rori held onto the steering wheel for dear life as the van jerked to the right. It slowed but didn't stop.

"It didn't work. Now what? What are we going to do?"

"Easy, Angel." She was afraid to look away from the road, terrified someone would step into the street and she'd hit them. She'd just had the van checked a week ago and everything was fine. How could this be happening?

"It was done deliberately."

"What?" She hadn't realized she'd spoken out loud, but he confirmed the thought that was running through her head. Who could hate her so much that they were trying to kill her?

"Stay calm, watch the road. Do you trust me?"

"Yes, of course."

"Good. When I tell you to turn right, don't think just do it."

"Okay." Her hands gripped the wheel so hard they started to cramp. It's when she realized she was almost standing on the brake pedal.

"Now. Turn now, Angel." Doing as he said,

she turned the wheel. The tires squealed on the pavement as the van took the turn much faster than it should have and slammed head-on into a huge steel dumpster.

The airbag deployed and her head slammed into the side window. Everything seemed fuzzy and she couldn't move but she was still alive.

"Jasper?"

"I'm here, Angel." His voice sounded far away, and her head throbbed like it was being pounded with a sledgehammer. "I'm here. Can you turn your head away from the window?"

She shifted over just enough to move away from the door allowing Jasper to pull it open. But she was pinned by the airbag and couldn't move much. "Is the cake okay?"

"Don't worry about the cake. We need to make sure you're okay."

"I'm fine, but Mrs. Evanston…"

"Shh, Angel. Let me get you out of there, then we'll worry about the cake." Carefully he slid his arms behind her back and gently pulled her from the seat. She didn't think she was injured except her head, where the drums were still pounding loud and clear. The impact against the window had been hard enough to shatter it.

"I hear sirens. Are they real?"

"They're real. I'd bet you have a concussion. I'm so sorry, Angel."

"Why are you sorry? I'm fine." He grunted but didn't put her down. Instead, he walked over to the curb and sat with her in his lap. Then he turned her face so he could look more closely at her head.

"You've got a nasty bruise forming already."

"Yeah, well you should see the other guy."

"I'm glad to see you still have your sense of humor. Does anything else hurt?"

"I don't think so. Maybe my chest a little, but it's probably from the airbag."

"Maybe. We'll get you checked out to make sure."

The sirens were closer and then they finally stopped. If they'd gotten any louder, her head would have imploded. The pain was excruciating, and her left eye refused to stay open.

"Are you okay?" Steele bent down to get a look at her. She'd seen him more in the last week than she had since she'd gotten back to Willow Haven. She should get up to explain what happened, but it was too comfortable in Jasper's arms, and with her head against his chest it didn't pound as much. He was warm and safe. Nope, she wasn't moving unless they made her.

~

"I'm fine, but Rori got banged up pretty bad. She needs to be checked out."

"The ambulance is on the way. They'll take her to Willow Haven Hospital."

Before he could say anything, Chase showed up. "What the hell happened? I thought you were supposed to be taking care of her?"

"I was. I'd bet a month's salary someone cut the brake line."

"We'll have it towed and look at it," Ethan said. "I'm shocked you guys are in one piece. It was brilliant turning into the alley."

"Yeah, but I couldn't keep Rori from being hurt."

"I'm fine, I keep telling you. But you can't take the cake," Rori mumbled.

"What is she talking about?" Chase asked, looking at Jasper for an explanation.

"We were delivering a wedding cake to Ruby's for the Evanston's vow renewal. She's more worried about the damn cake than herself."

"Where is it?"

"In the back of the van. It was secured pretty well, but I doubt it survived the collision with the dumpster."

Steele opened the back of the van and stepped back so Jasper could see. The cake's top slid off with the impact, but it didn't look too bad. He'd expected to see cake plastered all over the inside of the van.

"Let me see," Rori said as she squirmed to get up.

After all she'd put into it, he knew she'd drive herself crazy until she could see it. He helped her stand and supported her as she gingerly made her way to the van. His Angel was one stubborn woman.

"Oh no. It's ruined."

"Nah, it's just a little lopsided. I bet no one will even notice." When she turned to look at him, he winced. Anyone seeing her face would have figured she'd gone ten rounds and lost badly. Her left eye was swollen shut and it was hard to tell where her eye began, and her face ended. The whole left side was twice it's normal size and had turned a purple-red color. It was painful just to look at it. He couldn't imagine how much she was hurting.

"Let me try to fix it."

"How about you let Steele and Ethan deal with getting the cake to Ruby's and fixed up. You'll take care of it, right, guys?"

"Sure." But from the look on their faces, it was the last thing they wanted to do. There was no way Jasper was leaving Rori's side again. He'd had to do it in Paris, but not this time.

"Chase, I think it might have been the guy hanging around the bakery yesterday. The one in the video I sent over this morning."

"Alex is still working on trying to ID him. But maybe we'll get some prints from the van."

"Can you send it over to me, Chase. I'll need it for the official report," Steele asked.

"Yeah. No problem. But if we can't identify him, I doubt you can," Chase replied, never missing a chance to rib his brother.

"No, but if he did cut the brake line there might be prints, and it will help to have an ID for the APB. We'll tow it to the garage and see what we find."

"How much longer until the ambulance gets here?"

"I don't need to go to the hospital. Let's just go back to the apartment."

"Nope, you need to be checked out."

"I don't want to go."

"Humor me, Angel. You're pretty beat up." She tried to give him the stink eye, but with the condition of her face, it was plain pitiful. At least they'd both survived. His ribs were sore but nothing he couldn't handle. She'd taken the brunt of it, and he'd have given anything to prevent it. It was pure luck he saw the alley and the dumpster in time for her to take the turn. Only a collision would stop the van, and this had been the best possible solution. Sometimes that's all you got.

By now they had attracted quite a crowd. Surveilling the area, he saw the same guy who'd been in the bakery. With a nod of his head, he got Chase's attention and nodded in the direction of the man. He must have realized he'd been spotted because he took off with Chase and Ethan on his tail.

Jasper would have preferred to be the one chasing the dirtbag and take the guy apart piece by piece. In his gut, he knew that he'd been the one tormenting Rori, but they still had no idea why. But that would have to wait. For now, his first priority was to get her to the hospital.

The ambulance finally showed up and he rode with her. There was no way he was going to let her out of his sight. When they arrived, the nurse took them into one of the curtained areas and took her information. It was another fifteen minutes before the doctor made it in.

Jasper had to threaten Rori to keep her in the bed. The doctor took one look at her and ordered x-rays and a CT scan of her head, then made him step out while he examined her. He didn't want to leave, but if she wasn't safe there, she wouldn't be anywhere, and he left them to their work.

Twenty minutes later, the doctor came out to get him. "How is she?"

"She's got a concussion, bruised ribs, and bruising around her neck and shoulders from the seatbelt. Luckily there are no broken bones, but she's going to be in a lot of pain for a few days," he said as he walked Jasper back to her room.

"He wants me to stay overnight, but I told him you'd take care of me at home."

Jasper looked from Rori to the doctor and shrugged. He'd prefer to have her where he could watch over her, and if that's what she wanted he was okay with it.

"Tell me what I have to do. I've had some field medic training, and I'll make sure she follows your directions."

The doctor didn't look happy, but he knew a brick wall when he saw one. He wrote out a prescription for pain meds and the concussion protocol instructions.

"If anything changes or she vomits or anything else on that list, bring her back."

"I'll be fine, doctor."

"I'll make sure she follows your orders. I promise I'll take good care of her." The doctor gave him one more look and then left the room. "Now I have to figure out how to get you home."

"I can't believe this happened."

"I'm so sorry, Angel. I wish it was me in that

bed instead of you. If only I could have stopped it another way."

"I'm fine. In a couple of days you won't even be able to tell so stop it. You're not Superman, although you sure did a good impersonation last night. But you figured out the best solution to an impossible situation."

"I don't know. It sure as hell seems like I'm doing a piss poor job of protecting you."

"Don't be so hard on yourself. I don't know how you could have expected this," Chase said from the opening in the curtain. "I told the nurse I was your brother-in-law, so they let me in."

"Perfect timing. I was trying to figure out how to get her home."

"Faith and Lily are bringing over some food and meeting us at your place. There was no stopping them when they found out."

"They don't need to, especially Lily, she's due any day now." Jasper rolled his eyes. This was the second time she was in the middle of a clusterfuck, and all she ever did was worry about others.

"Don't worry about it. Alex will make sure she's fine. Oh, and I got the cake to the Evanston wedding. They were thrilled with it but are worried about you. You'll probably have all the little old ladies lining up as soon as you open the bakery again."

"I worked so damn hard on that cake. I can't believe it's ruined. Wait, what do you mean again? The bakery will be open tomorrow just like always."

"Why don't you wait and see how you feel in the morning before you decide."

"It was still beautiful. You should have heard all the oohs and ahhs when I carried it in."

"But…"

"No buts. C'mon, Angel. Let's get you home."

CHAPTER 16

Faith and Lily were waiting in the parking lot to help Rori as she got out of the car. It brought tears to her eyes. She felt so alone when she'd first returned. Even though Anna offered to help with anything, she just couldn't deal with anyone. Meeting Lily had been wonderful, and her friendship meant the world to her. She just hadn't realized how much until that moment. As much as her life had sucked the last few years, she still had a lot to be thankful for, and the people standing around her were the reason.

"Thank you, all of you for being here for me."

"Aww don't cry, Rori. It'll be okay the important part is that you're alive."

"I know. But for a few minutes there I didn't think I would be. I still don't know how you stayed so calm the entire time."

Jasper shrugged and looked at Chase, then back at her. "Years of training, Angel."

Faith nodded. "Chase is the same way. When I had my stalker in California, it was the same thing."

"Really?"

"Yeah, one of these days I'll tell you the gory details."

"How about we continue this upstairs. I'd just as soon get Rori off her feet and in a protected area."

"Yes, sir," Lily said with a laugh but took Rori's hand and helped her to the door.

Chase and Jasper held back a moment, and from the look on Jasper's face, it wasn't good news. Too bad she couldn't hear them.

"C'mon. We'll find out soon enough. Let's just get you inside and cleaned up. Oh yeah, that reminds me. Chase, can you grab the casserole dishes out of the truck."

Rori fished the keys out of her purse, and

Faith unlocked the door while Lily held on to her arm, but before they could step inside, Jasper was there.

"Let me go in first and look around. You stay with Chase. I'll be right back."

Rori mumbled under her breath, "you're kidding, right?"

"No, I'm not, Angel." He kissed her forehead and disappeared inside the building. True to his word he was back a few minutes later, and for the first time she noticed he was favoring his side. "We're good. Do you want me to carry you up?"

"No, I can do it myself. You're hurt." Could he be any more overprotective? But really, she couldn't fault him. He'd saved her life. Twice. And he called her angel? He had it all wrong, *he was her* guardian angel.

"I'm fine. It's nothing."

Just as the doctor warned, she was starting to hurt in places she didn't know existed. "Whatever. I think I need a hot shower."

"Are you sure? If you're dizzy, it might not be the best idea."

"I'll help her. Is that okay, Rori?" Faith asked after she exchanged looks with Lily. Being nine months pregnant made it hard for her to move around much too.

"Thank you. That'd be great, although I'm sure I'll be fine. I don't feel dizzy at all."

"If you guys throw the casseroles in the oven on three hundred fifty, they'll be ready to eat by the time she's all cleaned up."

As soon as they got to Rori's bedroom, Faith and Lily were full of questions. "So, I guess things are going well with the two of you? It's not so bad having a bodyguard after all, huh?"

"Hey, my head is killing me. One question at a time. And no, I'm not going to tell you everything, so just forget it. A lady doesn't kiss and tell."

"We can tell just from the way he looks at you. And you have that glow even though you're three shades of purple," Lily said.

"Yup. So maybe you need to open your eyes, err eye. I don't think you'll be opening that left one for a few days," Faith chimed in.

Rori turned to look in the mirror. "Oh my God." No wonder her head hurt. Half her face was swollen and bruised, and her eye was swollen shut. "I'm a horror story."

"No, you're not. Cut it out. You were in a car accident. You'll be fine in a few days."

"Because of Jasper." She didn't know how she would ever thank him. He'd been there for her on two of the worst days in her life. He said he wanted her, that he wasn't leaving. Had he really meant all the things he'd said to her last night? She needed to talk to him, but it wouldn't happen until they were alone. For now, she needed that shower. Maybe the heat would help the swelling.

"How come you didn't answer Alex's emails," Chase demanded as soon as they were alone.

"I didn't have a chance to read them yet. I was going to do it as soon as we got back from the delivery."

"He called me when he couldn't get in touch with you. Alex traced the source of the calls to Cynthia Marshall in Boston. Apparently, she's Jim's twin sister. She went off the deep end after he was killed in Paris."

"If she's in Boston then she's not the one causing all the trouble here."

"Alex is trying to find any connection between Cynthia and anyone local. And he's still working on trying to ID the guy in the video."

"Maybe we'll get lucky, and there will be a fingerprint on the brake line."

"Or he'll try again. If he meant to kill her, he isn't done."

"I know. My gut tells me it's the guy from the bakery, or that he's involved somehow. I haven't had a chance to ask Rori if she'd seen him before. I almost got her killed today."

"No, you didn't. There was nothing Alex turned up to indicate they'd tamper with her van. It was pure genius to have her drive into the dumpster. It could have been so much worse."

"I know. She was terrified when she realized the brakes were shot, but she listened and stayed calm. Did Alex find out anything else?"

"Alex thinks Cynthia is behind it all. She was in a private clinic after Jim's death, and from the records he dug up, she doesn't seem too stable."

"Alex is amazing on the computer."

"Yeah, which is why I pushed him so hard to come to work for us. I sure as hell don't want to know how he got private medical info, but I'm glad he did. But because it's not legal we can't share it with Ethan and Steele."

"Understood."

They continued to discuss plans and options. Jasper was convinced it was the guy from the bakery and he was itching to get his hands on him. He'd managed to get away from Chase and disappear, but he'd bet he was still hiding in town, waiting for his next opportunity.

"I think you both should come stay with us."

"No, we're not going anywhere. This is my home."

The two men turned to the three women standing in the kitchen doorway. They were ex-special teams, and yet the women managed to sneak up on them. Not a good sign at all. "I guess we're slipping, Chase. They could have taken us out before we knew they were there."

"Don't tempt me," Rori said with a smile. She looked a little better after her shower, but he winced when he looked at her swollen face and eye. He loved that she'd left her long brown curls loose instead of putting them up the way she usually wore her hair.

"I have to agree with Rori. I think we're better off here, besides I don't want to bring any trouble your way."

"It wouldn't be…Okay, but if anything else happens, I'm not taking no for an answer."

"If you he-men are done making all the decisions, how about we eat?" Faith said as she pushed past them to get to the stove.

"You made chicken Tetrazzini?"

"Yeah, I figured why not try it. My kitchen skills have improved tons since you've been helping."

"I can vouch for that."

"No one asked you. Unless you want to feel the burn of this dish I'd suggest you move." Faith smiled and brushed against Chase as she moved past him. Jasper envied their relationship, well not envy so much as wished for the same with Rori. But if he couldn't keep her safe he wasn't worthy of her love.

Dinner was delicious, even though he had no idea what chicken Tetrazzini was, he'd eat it again in a heartbeat.

"Thanks for bringing dinner, Faith. I'm

sorry I don't have anything to offer for dessert. Unless you want to go get something from the bakery? I need to get down there and clean and prep for tomorrow still."

"You don't need to worry about it. The bakery will be closed tomorrow. You'll make up for it in sales when you reopen. Everyone in town will want to hear what happened." He wasn't going to allow her to push herself. She needed rest and time to recuperate.

"But…"

"There you go with the buts again."

"I agree with Jasper. You should take a few days off at least. You're the only bakery in town you won't lose customers."

"I'd prefer you didn't open again until we figure out who's targeting you. Today proved they're serious and don't plan on letting up. You could have been killed." The last thing Jasper wanted to do was scare her, but she needed to listen so he could keep her safe.

"I'll give you tomorrow. But after that, we'll see."

"You are one stubborn woman."

"Only when it comes to something I care about." They'd said a lot of things the night before, but he wondered if she'd changed her mind after what happened today. More than anything he wanted to keep her safe and prove he was worthy of her love.

"Okay, c'mon Faith, let's bring Lily back to Alex and head home. If you need anything call, I can be here in about twenty minutes."

"Thanks, Chase. Faith, if you ever decide you want a new career you can come work at the bakery with me."

"No way. But thank you for the compliment."

The women hugged, and Chase gave Rori a kiss on the unbruised side of her forehead. "Talk to you tomorrow."

"I'll go down and lock up, you stay put, okay?"

"Yes, sir."

Jasper shook his head as he followed them downstairs.

"You better not hurt her," Lily said.

"What? I'd never hurt her."

"It's obvious she's fallen hard for you. Don't you dare break that girl's heart. She's already been through too much."

Chase looked as surprised as Jasper at Lily's comments.

"I don't plan on ever hurting her. I hope she'll have me, but I have to make sure she's safe first."

Lily nodded and smiled. Obviously hearing exactly what she was hoping. Jasper checked the lock on the bakery door, then locked the apartment entrance and headed upstairs to his angel.

CHAPTER 17

Rori was waiting for him in the living room when he got upstairs. She looked like she was ready to go to sleep, it didn't help that he'd had her up most of the night before. But she needed to be awake for a while longer because of the concussion protocols. "How are you feeling, can I get you anything?"

"I'm good."

"How about some coffee?"

"I don't think so. Can you sit with me?"

"I wish you would have let me fill the prescription for the pain pills. You're going to need them in the morning."

"I'll be fine. I hate those things they make me loopy."

"Tylenol?"

"Maybe in a bit. I want to talk." It was never a good thing when a woman said those words. It's one of the first things men learn.

"What do you want to talk about?" he asked as he sat next to her on the couch. She was leaning against one of the arms, and he picked up her feet and draped them over his lap. He rubbed one foot and then the other without even thinking about it. They were so tiny compared to his size thirteens.

"Mmm, that feels good. But don't try to distract me."

"I'm not." She was wearing leggings and a t-shirt, and with hair curling around her face and shoulders, she looked adorable. It brought back memories of the night before when he'd tangled his fingers in her hair as he'd made love to her. Just thinking about it gave him an erection. "What do you want to talk about, Angel?"

"I want to know what you and Chase were talking about. I know it was about me, and I have a right to know."

"I wasn't trying to keep anything from you. I was hoping to get more information first."

"What did you find out?"

"Did Jim ever tell you he had a twin sister?"

"He had a twin?"

"Yeah, and she took his death really hard. Her family had to commit her to a private facility for a while after he died. She's been in and out a few times since then."

"Oh wow, that's awful. But what does she have to do with me?"

"We're fairly sure she's the one behind the phone calls. Alex was able to trace them back to her."

"Why would she mess with me? I'm surprised she even knows who I am. I told you, I never met any of them."

"We figure she saw the piece in the paper about you and the bakery. In her twisted mind, she probably blames you for Jim's death."

"But that doesn't make any sense. It was a terrorist attack."

"It's probably easier to blame you. She's not stable so it doesn't have to make sense to us, just to her."

"But he was in Paris long before I got there."

"She's unbalanced and that makes her

dangerous. Honestly, I think she's behind every-thing that's been happening to you."

"Really? She's here? In Willow Haven?"

"Not that we can tell. We have proof she was in Boston yesterday but that doesn't mean she didn't hire someone to hurt you or worse. You could have been killed today. Probably would have been if I wasn't with you."

"But if she's not here…"

"If she hired someone she's just as culpa-ble." Worry wrinkled Rori's brow. He didn't want to keep information from her, but he hated upsetting her especially after all she'd been through already. She needed to be calm and not have extra stress.

"What do we do? What happens next?"

"We're trying to track her calls and movements. We'll keep an eye on her and see if she's been in contact with anyone local. There was a guy hanging around in a leather jacket and a hoodie yesterday that looked out of place and took off without buying anything. I saw him again as we pulled out of the parking lot to deliver the cake."

"Is that why you yelled stop?"

"Yup. I guess it was a good thing too, at least it kept you from stepping on the gas."

"You think he's involved?"

"I'm not sure but it looks like it. I saw him after the accident and Chase tried to catch him, but he got away. That's too many coincidences."

Nodding, she chewed on her lower lip and stared at the wall. The wheels were definitely turning, and he'd give anything to know what she was thinking.

"Maybe she's right, and it is my fault. If Jim hadn't proposed then he'd still be alive."

"You don't know that. Don't let his sister put thoughts in your head. He was a grown man able to make his own decisions. No one twisted his arm. It was just bad luck that you were all there that night."

"I know, and intellectually I agree, but my heart doesn't."

"It's the same for us if we lose a teammate.

He put her foot down and slowly ran his hand along her leg and under the leggings until he reached the scarring from the bullet wounds.

"It feels weird, right?"

"Not really, mine's worse. Does it still hurt?"

"Sometimes, mostly on wet, humid days."

"Mine too."

"Will you tell me what happened? How did you get the scar on your face? Did it happen the same time your leg was injured?"

"My last mission was a total clusterfuck. I can't tell you much, it's classified, but I lost a good friend. I had substantial injuries, and two surgeries on my thigh. But I'm better, just not good enough to go back to my team."

"I'm sorry."

"It's okay. It's my own fault, I was distracted." He wouldn't tell her he'd been thinking about her. It had been his own fault. After Paris, his mind wasn't on point like it should have been. Whenever he had downtime his mind wandered thinking about her. Wondering what she was doing, if she was happy. No matter what he'd done he couldn't get her out of his head.

"I'm still sorry. You were wonderful in Paris. I know I wouldn't be here if you hadn't come when you did. That's twice you've saved me."

"Just doing my job."

"After last night, is it still just *your job*? I was hoping we'd moved beyond that." What was she asking?

"I meant what I said last night. I want you. All of you. I never say anything I don't mean."

"Good, because nothing has changed for me. I want you, Jasper. I need you. I don't want you to leave when this is settled. I want to see if we can have a life together."

"Are you sure? Because once you're mine, I'm not letting you go. I can't. Not after spending two years trying to find you."

"I've never been more certain of anything. I know it's fast, but it feels like it's our destiny and I won't deny it. I don't want to risk losing you."

It was sheer will power that kept him in check. She was hurting, bruised, broken. Making love to her was out of the question. Instead, he scooped her into his arms and carried her to the bedroom. After pulling the comforter aside, he placed her on the bed and climbed in next to her, still fully dressed. The barrier of his clothing helped him hold on to his control. If he felt her skin against his, he'd be toast.

"Rori, are you really sure?"

"Yes, I want you so much it hurts."

He'd hate himself in the morning if he caused her any more pain. He understood her need, her desire, he just prayed he had the strength to maintain his control.

Gently, he settled her against his side and kissed her. Softly sliding his lips across hers. Damn, she always tasted so sweet. He drank her in, pouring all his love into the kiss.

Desire burned him from the inside out. He craved the feel of her skin against his, to take her again and again until neither of them could think. But when he helped her remove her t-shirt it was like he poured ice water on his libido. Bruises painted her chest from the airbag and seatbelt and matched the ones on her face. How was she not in terrible pain? "I don't want to hurt you, Angel."

"You won't, please, baby. I need you inside me. I want us to be so close nothing can get between us."

He stood and removed his shirt but left his jeans on. His willpower was not bottomless, but if she wanted him, she'd get him, just not all.

Climbing onto the bed, he straddled her legs and slowly, gently pulled her leggings off, like he was unwrapping an expensive piece of chocolate.

"I'm going to love every inch of you."

She blushed, and it traveled from her cheeks, down her neck, and across her chest. Last night she'd been glowing in the moonlight, today she was bruised and battered and even though she tried to hide it, she was in pain. He'd just have to make sure that her passion distracted her from anything but him.

Whoever invented front closure bras should get some kind of an award. It was a life saver as he opened the hooks and exposed her two gorgeous globes. Her mauve nipples were already hard little peaks. Last night had only whetted his appetite, he'd never have his fill. This was so much better than he ever could have imagined.

Her skin was soft, like rose petals, and tasted of vanilla and sugar. Teasing each of her nipples with his teeth and tongue until her moans filled him with need. She was a goddess and he would happily spend the rest of his life loving every inch of her.

CHAPTER 18

Every lick, each nibble along her skin pushed her closer to the edge of the abyss. His mouth, his tongue, his fingers, played her body like she was a fine instrument. She ached for him, her core soaked and quivering, needing to be filled, but he refused. It was maddening.

"Jasper, baby, please. I need you."

"You have me, Angel. But not today. You need to be treasured, we'll have our time, but tonight is all about you."

"But…"

"What did I tell you about those buts? Let me love you, Rori, let me satisfy your desires."

"Oh God, this is torture."

"No, Angel, this is love." After that, there were no more words. He slid her soaked panties off and parted her thighs. Then he blew on her most private parts and fanned the flames of her desire. She thought she'd die of embarrassment as he stared at her. Then he slid his finger inside and when he pulled it out it glistened with her essence. Watching him slip his finger into his mouth and close his eyes, had to be one of the sexiest things she'd ever seen. He was going to be the death of her.

Licking his lips, he slid between her legs and when his tongue touched her most sensitive spot, she arched off the bed. Bright lights flashed in her eyes as her body shuddered and tightened, as he continued to lick, suck and nibble.

As she came, she cried out, moaning his name like a mantra over and over, as she rode the waves of pleasure. The heart-pounding release left her feeling boneless like a ragdoll.

Jasper moved up the bed and pulled her against him to cuddle. "Are you okay?"

"Oh, my God, yes. I thought last night was intense but seeing you, it was just wow."

"What do you mean? I didn't do anything different than last night."

"I know, but last night was in the dark, and it seemed more intense. And well, Jim never—" her voice trailed off, she couldn't bring herself to say it. She wasn't a prude, but sex wasn't something she discussed with anyone.

"I'm sorry to hear that, he didn't know what he was missing."

"When can we do it again?"

Jasper laughed and pulled her closer. "After you've gotten some rest. You're supposed to stay calm. I doubt the doctor would say multiple orgasms is keeping you calm. I am looking forward to teaching you so many things. But you need to heal first. Then you can really enjoy it."

"But you didn't…"

"I told you, this was about you. I meant what I said last night. You will always come first."

Joy filled her to overflowing, but there was sadness as well, for what would never be. Jasper made her complete in ways Jim never had, maybe he'd never been the right person for her. But would he be willing to settle down in one place when he was used to traveling the world? Pushing the thoughts from her head, she focused on the feel of his arms around her, the beat of his heart against her cheek, and the love filling her to the brim.

"Can I get you anything? Some water? Food?"

"Water and a Tylenol would be great."

"I knew you should have filled that script."

"No, it's not bad, except for the pounding in my head. I'm really fine."

"Hell yeah, you are, better than fine, and you better never forget it."

Would she ever stop blushing when he said stuff like that? She loved how open he was, and how concerned about her wellbeing beyond the call of duty. But it was more, she loved him. There was no way to protect her heart, she'd given it to her protector.

He'd just walked back into her room with the glass of water when the building shook and a loud blast echoed through the apartment. It felt like an earthquake and almost knocked Jasper off his feet.

"What the fuck? I'm going to check the cameras. Can you get dressed without help?"

"Yes, but it will take longer than usual."

"That's okay, just don't leave the apartment unless you smell smoke, or I come for you. Okay?"

"Where are you going?"

"To catch the motherfucker. He's going to learn what it means to mess with my woman."

"Please don't go. Let's just call Steele and Ethan."

"Call Chase instead, I'm sure someone already called the police. I'll be right back. Don't worry. I love you, Angel."

Then he was gone. She hadn't even had a chance to tell him she loved him too. Please, God, don't let anything happen to him. It was a struggle, but she got dressed, slowly pulling on her discarded clothing. Then her phone rang. It was Lily. The only reason she'd call is if something was wrong with the baby.

"Lily? What's wrong?"

"Nothing yet, but if you don't come outside now, you'll never see your friend alive again." It was the same disguised voice as the other phone calls. Then she heard a woman's scream and it terrified her.

"Where do I need to go?"

"The parking lot out back. And don't stop to

let your boyfriend know or your friend won't be breathing any longer." Jasper was going to kill her when he found her gone, but she couldn't handle losing another person she cared about.

"Don't hurt her."

"That's up to you."

What had she done to cause this? She tried to be kind to everyone, but someone hated her enough that they kept trying to rip her life apart thread by thread. Tears clouded her vision as she slowly made her way down the stairs. She said a silent prayer that it would all work out, that Jasper would find her before anything bad happened. That he'd save her and Lily. He promised and she believed him.

The bakery was engulfed in flames by the time Jasper got downstairs to see what had happened. The brick building had kept it from spreading, but it would only be a matter of time. He had to get Rori out of there, but he needed to make sure no one was still inside. The heat was staggering. As he pulled open the door, he jumped back in case there was a backdraft from the fire, or another explosion. The sirens were getting louder which meant the firefighters were on the way. Whether they'd arrive in time to save the bakery was debatable.

Barefoot and only in jeans, he grabbed the fire extinguisher inside the bakery door and worked on the fire. He was hoping to keep it contained until the fire trucks arrived. The heat scorched his skin and made it difficult to breathe. Glass was strewn across the floor and cut his feet, but he had to make sure no one was inside the burning building.

Grabbing one of the towels Rori used to dry dishes, he ran it under water to dampen it, then held it over his face while using the extinguisher to make a path through the flames from the kitchen into the front of the bakery. The smoke was thick and billowing out of the front where the broken plate glass window had been. But replacing it again was going to be the least of Rori's problems. It was difficult to make out much of anything in all the smoke but there was a piece of something on the floor that didn't look like it belonged. Grabbing it and tucking it into his pocket, he made his way back through the bakery and outside.

"Fucking son of a bitch," Jasper cursed as he gasped for breath and rubbed watery eyes. He made it back outside in time for Chase to pull up.

"What the fuck happened?

"I think someone tossed a Molotov cocktail through the front window. There's no other logical explanation. I went through the place to make sure it was empty, and I found this." Jasper held out the broken piece of a wine bottle with the remnants of a charred label. "Definitely not something you'd find in Rori's bakery."

"Do you have a death wish? Going into a burning building like that? What were you thinking?"

"I wasn't. It was more instinct than anything."

"Where's Rori?"

"Upstairs. It's only been about five minutes since I got down here. I told her to stay put until I got back and asked her to call you."

"But she didn't call. I got an alert on my phone. I had Alex set it up after the window incident. If there is any police activity at this address I know about it."

"It would have been nice if you told me that before."

"You were here so it didn't matter. Backup should be here any second. You can wait and brief them. Besides, your feet are bleeding. You should get them checked out when the ambulance gets here. I'll go get Rori."

"Okay." Jasper leaned against Chase's truck and tried to breathe through the smoke that had clogged his lungs. He should have thought twice before going into the building. If someone had been in the bakery, it probably was whoever started the fire, and they deserved what they got.

"Did you leave the door unlocked? She's not there."

"Fuck no. Do you think I'm an asshole? How can she not be there? Did you check everywhere?"

"Yeah. Both doors were unlocked, the outside access and the apartment. There's no sign of her."

"Fuck me running. I have to be the world's shittiest bodyguard. But it was only five minutes and she was locked up tight, and she should have been safe inside. I promised her I wouldn't let anyone hurt her again."

"She couldn't have gone far. Like you said, it's only been about five minutes. She knew she was supposed to stay inside."

"You said she didn't call you? She was grabbing the phone as I left the apartment, so who did she call?

A terrified scream filled the air. Rori. "Do you see her? Where did that come from?"

"Over there, look." Chase pointed toward the parking lot behind the adjacent building.

If it wasn't for Rori's white t-shirt they wouldn't have seen them in the encroaching darkness. Two figures had her and were pulling her across the lot. There was a dark van and it had to be where they were dragging her toward.

Without a word, Jasper took off at a dead run even though his lungs felt like they were going to explode. After circling around the building, he approached the soon to be dead men from behind. The fucktards didn't have a chance, they just didn't know it yet. Delta always completed their missions or died trying.

"Let her go."

"What?" The one guy holding Rori turned toward him, and Jasper saw the gun shoved into her side. "Fuck you, asshole. I'm the one with a gun."

"You don't want to mess with him, he'll kill you even without a gun," Rori said, her voice about ten octaves higher than usual.

"Bitch, don't make me tell you again to shut the fuck up."

Jasper was weighing his options. The fucker with the gun was closest to him, but the other one nearer the van was an unknown. If he had a gun he might shoot Rori before he could take them both out.

Falling back on years of training, the world seemed to slow down, and he looked from one man to the other. Rori was safe as long as he kept her from being pushed into the van. He needed a distraction, and he got his wish a few heartbeats later as the fire trucks roared into the lot.

It was all he had to hear. Jasper moved so quickly the guy never saw it coming. They were distracted by the sirens and flashing lights, and it gave him just enough time to take him out. Grabbing the hand with the gun, he spun him around, and disarmed him, before punching him in the side of the head. He went down, but not until Jasper had pushed Rori behind him.

"Jasper, watch out."

He turned in time to see a lead pipe coming for his head. He reached for asshole number one's gun and he shot dirtbag number two in the arm. The pipe hit the asphalt with a loud clang just as Chase caught up to them. He grabbed the guy and shoved him up against the side of the van.

"I hope you feel like talking because we have a lot of questions for you, asshole," Chase growled.

Once they had the situation under control, Rori threw herself into Jasper's arms.

"Are you okay, Angel? Did they hurt you? Later you and I are going to have a talk about what stay put means."

"I'm fine. They didn't hurt me, but I think I need to look into some martial arts training for next time."

"There better not be a next time."

Chase nodded and grabbed his asshole and dragged him over to Ethan and Steele who were headed their way.

"Thank you for saving me again. This is becoming a habit."

"Angel, you're my life. I love you. I think I have from the first night in Paris. But I failed you. I'm so sorry." His breathing still hadn't returned to normal. He was covered in smoke and his feet were bleeding, but he'd never been happier in his life. Holding Rori in his arms and knowing she was safe was all he needed.

"You're not responsible for my actions. You have never failed me, not one time. I never want to hear you say those words again. I love you, Jasper."

He held her as tightly as he dared with all of her injuries and took her lips in a demanding kiss. When they came up for air, he rested his forehead against hers and sighed. She'd said the words he'd longed to hear. He had a chance for a new beginning, they both did, and he would do his best to make sure she got the happily ever after she deserved. "Thank you for trusting me with your heart, your life, your future. I will cherish it for as long as I live."

CHAPTER 19

The ambulance finally arrived, and Jasper insisted they check Rori, she'd been through hell in the last twenty-four hours. The doctor would have his ass in a sling if he realized how "stress-free" her life had been. After they gave her the all-clear, she insisted he let them make sure he was okay.

"I'm fine. I've been through much worse."

"You're still coughing. Let them take a look at your feet if nothing else. Please. For me," she pleaded as she squeezed his hand. Life would never be boring around her, that's for sure and she already had him wrapped around her finger.

"Fine." Jasper gave in as he climbed into the ambulance for the EMTs to check him out.

While they looked at his feet to determine if he needed treatment, he had a few questions for her. "You know I can't turn you down. But dammit woman, now you need to tell me why you left the apartment. And why didn't you call Chase like I asked you to?"

"I was going to, but it rang before I had a chance to call him. I thought it was Lily, it was her number. When I answered it all I could hear was crying and then a man's voice telling me if I didn't come outside they would kill her. She's one of my best friends. I didn't know what else to do?"

"It showed up as her number?"

"Yeah.

"They must have cloned her phone. But still, didn't you think it might be a trap?"

"Of course, but I couldn't risk it. She's like fifty months pregnant, what if she really was in trouble? What would you have done in my shoes?"

It was a typical ploy and one that took more effort than just a couple of assholes being paid to harass her. But Rori was right, he'd have done what they'd asked, but he was a professional, trained for this.

Whoever was behind this whole thing had brains and money, or some damn good connections. It all led them back to Jim's sister and he hoped Alex had made some headway there.

"I would have done the same thing, but it's different."

"Why? Because you're a guy?"

"No, because I am Delta and not dealing with a concussion and bruised ribs among other things."

"I'll give you that. I guess. But it worked out okay."

"Because we got lucky. I was terrified they'd get you into that van and do God knows what to you."

"But they didn't. You saved me. See, all good," Rori said and she spun around like a little girl. Except she forgot about the concussion and almost fell over. Jasper hopped out of the ambulance and caught her before she could fall and hurt herself further.

"Apparently, saving you is going to be a full-time job for the rest of my life."

"Very funny."

"You both good? Have the police cleared

you to leave?" Chase asked as he walked up to Jasper.

"We're fine. What's up?" Jasper had hoped he'd be able to take Rori to a hotel room and relax for a bit before they had to deal with anything else.

"Alex called. Lily's in labor."

"Is she okay?" Rori asked. The part of her face that wasn't swollen and purple, had a worried expression.

"Apparently, she's used curse words no one in the hospital has heard before."

"Sounds like she's fine."

"Chloe and Logan are already at the hospital, so is Faith and probably everyone who works at ESP. I'm heading over, want a ride?"

"Thanks, that'd be great. Let me just run upstairs and put on more clothing and my sneakers. It also reminds me that I'm going to have to get a new vehicle."

"What about your Harley?" Chase called after him as he disappeared into the building. Five minutes later he was back and answered his question as they made their way to his SUV.

"I can't take Rori around on that."

"Why not," she asked.

"How will we deliver your wedding cakes? Who knows how long your van will be with the police?"

"Yeah, and who knows when my bakery will reopen. I've never been on a motorcycle. I'm up for it. But my car is at my parent's house. We can always use that for now."

"We'll see," Jasper said as he wrapped her seatbelt around her and gave her a kiss. "But not until after you're feeling better."

R ori was so excited she could barely contain it. Lily and Alex had been trying for so long to have a baby and now it was about to happen. They'd gotten close over the last six months when Lily's cravings for sweets had her visiting the bakery on a daily basis. Sometimes she'd come in with Chloe and her baby, Andy, but mostly she'd stop by midmorning and they'd chat when there was a lull in customers.

As they walked into the waiting area, it was a madhouse. Chase had been right, everyone who knew Alex and Lily, or at least it seemed like it, had piled into the small maternity ward waiting room, even Alex's service dog, Hunter. Chloe said that Alex had tried to get him into the delivery room, but the doctor wasn't having it.

"Rori, how are you? Chase told me what happened."

"I'm fine, unfortunately, the bakery isn't. Thank God Jasper and Chase were there." Saying the words out loud brought tears to her eyes. But she'd rebuild and she was sure Jasper would help. It was just a building, they'd survived. That's what really mattered.

"Well if you want to talk let me know."

"Thanks, I really appreciate the offer." Rori had forgotten that Faith was a psychologist and had been through her own living hell with a stalker. Jasper knew the story but said it was hers to tell.

After what seemed like hours, Alex walked through the doorway, exhausted but with a huge grin on his face. "It's a boy and a girl. Mom and babies are doing great. I am going to need to grow extra arms."

"Twins?" Rori laughed. No wonder Lily was so huge, and she'd kept dodging her questions about whether or not she knew the sex of the baby. They'd kept it a secret from everyone, including Chloe, Lily's bestie. She looked shell-shocked but happy.

"Well look at you with that super sperm," Rock responded. He was the other computer genius at ESP.

"Fuck, Rock, there are women here," Chase admonished.

"So? That's what equality is, right? Not like they don't know what sperm are. Take a chill pill, Boss man."

Jasper leaned over and whispered to Rori, "he's going to pay for that. Chase will have him working midnights for weeks." She couldn't help giggling. Looking around the room it was like one big family, and with Jasper at her side, it was filling her heart to overflowing. If they caught the person behind her stalking, then everything would be wonderful.

"Are you feeling okay? You look a little wobbly, Angel."

"I'm good. Really, really good." She squeezed his hand and smiled. For the first time, it was the whole truth.

～

It didn't take Rori long to get her wish. Jasper's phone buzzed in his pocket and after checking the caller he gave Rori a kiss. "I need to take this outside. Will you be okay?"

"We'll make sure she has whatever she needs," Faith said.

"I'll be fine, go take care of whatever it is." She softened her words with a smile and another squeeze of his hand.

"I'll be right back."

The reception was horrible inside the hospital and he wouldn't have been able to hear. Once he was outside, Jasper returned the call. "Hey, Steele, you called?"

"I thought you'd want to know that the two guys flipped on Cynthia Marshall as soon as we got them into custody. They were like two freakin' canaries."

"Seriously? I guess she royally fucked up when she hired those two fucktards."

"That's what Ethan said. All we had to say was attempted murder and they were blaming each other and then Cynthia."

"Does that mean this ordeal is over for Rori?"

"It sure looks like it. But we don't have Cynthia in custody yet. The captain has a friend who's a Massachusetts State Trooper and she called up there and then sent the arrest warrant. They'll let us know when she's been apprehended."

"Excellent. I hope they get her quick. I don't want to tell Rori it's over until we know for sure."

"Oh yeah, and the crime scene techs were able to recover partials and at least one full fingerprint on the cut brake line. Good call on that."

"Thanks. I'm still kicking myself that I didn't notice when I moved the van to load up the cake."

"There was probably enough fluid left that it didn't affect it."

"Maybe. Hey, did you hear Lily gave birth to twins?"

"I did. My brother sent me a text when Alex let you all know."

"Did you update him on the case?"

"Hell no. You're the bodyguard and you

delivered all the clues. I shouldn't even be telling you, but I wanted you to rest easier tonight. I don't think Cynthia will pull anything else even if we don't get her into custody."

"I appreciate it and I know Rori does too."

"No problem. I'll let you know when we have Marshall in custody. Hopefully sooner than later."

"No shit. Take care."

Letting out a slow sigh of relief that it was close to done and his Angel would be safe, he jumped when her arms slid around his waist. He must be getting old, tired, or something, to let anyone sneak up on him.

"What do I do too?"

"How long have you been eavesdropping?"

"Long enough to know you were talking about me and the case. Did something happen? Did the guys confess?"

"Fuck yeah they did and gave up Jim's sister. She's the only piece not complete, but Steele said he'd give us a call when they had her in custody in Massachusetts."

"Is she definitely there? I worry she's going to show up here and do something even worse."

"She was there as of this morning. Alex has

been keeping tabs on her or had until he and Lily ended up having two babies today. Rock is probably still monitoring for him."

"But that was this morning, she could be here already."

"She's not." He pulled her around to face him and tipped her chin so he could look into her one good eye. "I know I haven't had the best track record, but this time I'm ninety-nine point nine percent sure that she's still up north. Okay?"

"Okay." Closing her eyes, she leaned against his chest, and it was her turn to sigh. It had been non-stop crazy for the past couple of months but with any luck, he'd have a phone call soon to tell him it was finished once and for all.

"Do you want to go back upstairs and see the babies?" Jasper asked as he led her back inside the hospital. Until that bitch was caught, he didn't want her outside with no protection.

"Yeah. Although I got to see them while you were down here. They're the most beautiful little people I've ever seen."

"Do they have names yet?"

"Alex won't tell us. I think they just enjoy torturing their friends."

"It wouldn't surprise me one bit."

"Everything okay?" Chase asked.

"Yeah, but I'm thinking about getting Rori to a hotel so she can rest."

"Why can't we go back to the apartment?"

"Because until the Fire Marshall clears it, we don't know if it's safe. The fire did a lot of damage."

"But all my stuff is in there." The stress was wearing on her again, and her voice got higher.

"Angel, it's okay. We'll get it, but we can't stay there yet."

"Okay, but instead of a hotel, how about we stay at my parent's house?"

"I didn't know you still had it," Chase said.

"Yeah, I couldn't stay there alone, but I couldn't bring myself to sell it yet either."

"Okay, we can do that," Jasper said. "But first let's go see the babies." He gave Chase a brief nod to let him know everything was okay, and they went to visit the nursery.

Alex was looking at his children with Hunter when they got there. It's like the dog understood what was going on. Staring through the window of the nursery at the two newest Barretts was completely awe inspiring. The babies were beautiful and a good size for twins. Rori said it was amazing they'd gone full term since so many twins are born early.

"Congratulations. Twins, too. You're going to be up to your eyeballs in dirty diapers."

Hunter woofed and they laughed.

"That's for damn sure. But I wouldn't miss it for anything."

"I should record that. I bet in about three months you'll have changed your tune."

"No way." Jasper envied him a little, as he gazed at his children and rubbed Hunter's head, apparently a service dog could go everywhere except the delivery room. He'd been through a lot to get there, but it seemed like most of the guys at ESP had. It was time for him to settle down too.

"So are you going to tell us their names?" Rori asked.

"Emma and Henry, and we're hoping you will be Henry's godmother, Rori. Chloe and Logan will be Emma's godparents."

"Oh my God, I'd love to. I'd be honored. Thank you."

"If you're sticking around, Lily and I would like you to be Henry's godfather."

"Are you sure? You don't know me very well."

"Lily insisted, said you made Rori happy again and that made you the perfect person."

Jasper was more than surprised. It was the last thing he'd expected. "Well, then I'd be happy to."

"Great. Now that it's all settled, get the hell out of here so I can spend time with my new family."

When they got downstairs, Chase and Faith were waiting to take them by the apartment and then to her parent's house. Jasper kept hoping his phone would ring with the word they'd nabbed Cynthia. But so far there hadn't been anything at all.

He helped Rori change the sheets on the bed and air out the house. Then he called and ordered another pizza since she'd enjoyed it so much and he couldn't remember the last time either of them had eaten.

His phone rang just after the pizza was delivered. His first instinct was to thank God, but then what if it was bad news.

"Hey Steele, what's up?"

"It's done. She was hiding out at her family's summer house on Martha's Vineyard. If it wasn't for one of the maids we probably wouldn't have found her. Her family was trying to get her to South America."

"Mother fuckers. I mean I guess I can understand not wanting to lose both children, but she almost killed Rori, and if we hadn't gotten the van to stop who knows how many others too."

"You're preaching to the choir. But at least Rori can sleep tonight knowing it's finally finished."

"Thanks. I appreciate all the help."

Rori was sitting more patiently than he would have under the circumstances, but maybe she'd already figured it out.

"They got her. It's over, Angel. You're safe."

"Thank God."

EPILOGUE

T hree months later...

R ori stood out front of the new and improved Prince's Patisserie, newly rebuilt and ready for the grand re-opening tomorrow. She'd been baking up a storm once they got the final sign-offs on all the inspections. Who knew it was worse to rebuild then start from scratch? Jasper, true to his promise, had been there every step of the way. Even asking Chase to keep him on local jobs if possible.

They'd gotten word a few weeks earlier that Jim's parents had begged for mercy for their daughter after she was found guilty, pleading with the court that she was mentally unstable. Rori felt sorry for them but the woman was a danger to those around her. So she hadn't been upset at all when Cynthia Marshall was sentenced to ten years in a medical facility for the criminally insane. It was even better that it was in Massachusetts. If she never met the woman it would be too soon as far as she was concerned. Although there were times in the middle of the night when she was cuddled up against Jasper that she realized if it hadn't been for her they'd never have found each other again.

He'd been working on fixing up her parent's house in his free time. They figured they'd keep it for when they had a family someday. He hadn't proposed yet, but Rori and Lily had a little side bet going that it would be soon.

"It looks perfect, Rori. You and Jasper did a great job."

"For a while there I didn't think we'd ever reopen."

"I knew it would work out."

"I know, that's what you kept telling me."

"I'm glad you kept the name. I was wondering if you'd change it."

"Jasper and I talked about it, but he said it was my baby and I could call it whatever I wanted. My parents made it possible, so I wanted to keep the name."

"I hope you baked enough for when you open the doors, I have a feeling you're going to be packed."

"I don't think I could fit anything else in the cases, I even have overflow in the back."

"What's Jasper up to?"

"I'm not sure, he was upstairs working on something. Probably getting into more trouble on Petfinder. He's determined to get a dog."

"Dogs, houses, new job, I'd say he's settled in pretty well."

"I had my doubts in the beginning, but he is a man of his word."

"Rori?"

"Speaking of the devil."

Jasper was hanging out of the upstairs window. Lily laughed.

"What's up?"

"Can you come up here?"

"I'll be right there."

"Give me a call later, I'm going to head

home. I'm sure Alex and Hunter are ready for a break from Henry and Emma by now."

"Thanks for your help getting the bakery ready for tomorrow."

"My pleasure, I hope it means lots of discounts in my future," Lily said as she waved and headed to her car.

Rori found Jasper sitting at the dining room table. "What's up, my sexy jack of all trades?"

"I have something for you."

"What is it?"

"This." He lifted a single cupcake off the table and handed it to her. It was pitiful and adorable. He'd gotten the consistency of the frosting all wrong, and it dripped down the side. She'd been teaching him how to cook and bake too. It had kept her busy while the bakery was under construction. And he'd taught her other things, like how to make love at least fifty different ways, in positions she'd never believed possible. But mostly he proved his love to her every day.

"Thank you. It's umm…beautiful."

"I know it's not up to your standards, but it's my first attempt and totally from scratch. I got the recipe off of Pinterest. That website is unbelievable. There's so much stuff, I wasn't sure which recipe to try. They all looked so good."

"Why didn't you ask me for one of mine?"

"Because I wanted to surprise you. Plus, if I asked you would have wanted to help and that would have defeated the purpose."

"I'm surprised you even know about Pinterest."

"I'm a man, but I do pay attention occasionally. I've heard you and Lily talking about how you can find just about anything on there. Aren't you going to try it?"

The hopeful look in his hazel eyes squeezed her heart. There wasn't a thing she'd deny him if it was in her power. Everything she'd been through was worth it to have found him, and he'd shown her the true meaning of love.

"Of course." Carefully, she peeled the paper wrapper off the side, and took a big bite and hit something hard. As she pulled the cupcake from her mouth, whatever she'd bitten into fell into her hand and was covered in cake and frosting. When she realized what it was, tears welled in her eyes. The heart-shaped diamond ring took her breath away. Only Jasper would have gone through so much trouble to make this so perfect.

"My dearest angel, will you do me the honor of becoming my wife and making my dreams come true?" Looking up from the ring at the sound of his voice, she saw that he was on one knee on the floor. Tears of happiness slid down her cheeks as she answered him.

"Yes, oh yes, Jasper."

"I love you, Angel."

"And I love you, my hero."

When they came up for air they were both covered in frosting and cake as he slipped the ring onto her finger.

ABOUT THE AUTHOR

Lynne St. James is the author of eighteen books in romantic suspense, contemporary and new adult romance. She lives in the mostly sunny state of Florida with her husband, an eighty-five-pound, fluffy, Dalmatian-mutt horse-dog, a small Yorkie-poo, and an orange tabby named Pumpkin who rules them all.

When Lynne's not writing about second chances and conquering adversity with happily ever afters, she's drinking coffee and reading or crocheting.

Where you can find Lynne:

Email: lynne@lynnestjames.com
Amazon: https://amzn.to/2sgdUTe
BookBub:
https://www.bookbub.com/authors/lynne-st-james
Facebook:

https://www.facebook.com/authorLynneStJames

Website: http://lynnestjames.com

Instagram: https://www.instagram.com/lynnestjames/

Pinterest: https://www.pinterest.com/lynnestjames5

VIP Newsletter sign-up: http://eepurl.com/bT99Fj

OTHER BOOKS BY LYNNE ST. JAMES

Black Eagle Team

SEAL's Spitfire: Special Forces: Operation Alpha, Book 1

SEAL's Passion: Special Forces: Operation Alpha, Book 2
(July 2019)

Beyond Valor

A Soldier's Gift, Book 1

A Soldier's Forever, Book 2

A Soldier's Triumph, Book 3

A Soldier's Protection, Book 4

A Soldier's Pledge, Book 5

A Soldier's Destiny, Book 6

A Soldier's Homecoming, Book 7 (TBD)

A Soldier's Redemption, Book 8 (TBD)

Raining Chaos

Taming Chaos

Seducing Wrath

Music under the Mistletoe – A Raining Chaos Christmas

(Novella)

Tempting Flame

Anamchara

Embracing Her Desires

Embracing Her Surrender

Embracing Her Love

The Vampires of Eternity (Not available)

Twice Bitten Not Shy

Twice Bitten to Paradise

Twice Bitten and Bewitched

Want to be one of the first to learn about Lynne St. James's new releases? Sign up for her newsletter filled with exclusive VIP news and contests!
http://eepurl.com/bT99Fj